The Day

God

Came to

Earth

Story by

Javonne Cupido

Written by

Aileen Friedman

ISBN – 13   978-0-620-68628-0

"It's a great book, a quick read, and it left you breathless and
stunned at the end. Thank God I'm saved!" – Susan Pottberg

About the author

Aileen Friedman is an accomplished author with several published novels, short stories, and children's books. Ms. Friedman taps into her personal experiences for inspiration, and her work has been very well-received throughout the world, for its accessibility and the believable characters she creates. Having been a dedicated Christian since 1987 and enduring all of life's tragedies, Ms. Friedman's stories carry a message of hope for all her readers.

Ms. Friedman left her home in South Africa and now lives in Mexico sharing God's word.

Philippians 4:13 "I can do all things through Christ who strengthens me."

Javonne Cupido

cupido.javonne@gmail.com

***

Aileen Friedman

Website
http://aileenfriedman.co.za

Facebook
https://www.facebook.com/groups/353447231333743/

Twitter
@aileenlf

Email
aileen2462@gmail.com

***

Book Cover Design
Simon Hattingh
seamonkey_studios@outlook.com

Table of Contents

From
Javonne Cupido

"To God, through whom all things are possible
and to
whom all glory is worthy,
this book has been completed.
In spite of worldly lack of support, I believe that
many souls will be saved through this book

***

From
Aileen Friedman

Thank you, Lord Jesus,
for your love and mercy
and for blessing me
with my family whom I love so much.
I am truly blessed.

Phil 4:13 'I can do all things through Christ who strengthens
me.'

***

A very special
THANK YOU
to
Susan Pottberg
For her support and for taking the time
to read this book and offer her
honest criticism.
For being a wonderful inspiration
to everyone that knows her and
that are in her presence.
We are forever grateful to know you.

Chapter One

Great expectation hung electrified amid the walls of the network studios, the stage, and editing, and recording rooms. The people scurried from one point to the next fearing the time will dissipate before they accomplished their designated task. From the high perches of the network owner to the low stance of the janitor; they all positively knew this breakout live TV entertainment talk show was going to be the greatest success of all TV talk shows.

To their credit, the network – SA9 – had snapped up the most sought after and highly paid TV show host of all time, Jonathan Bale.

A self-made story of success and wealth, Jonathan started his career as a journalist for a small town magazine in the Midlands of Kwa-Zulu Natal. His stories covered the desperate times of the rural families trying to cope with the modernization of teenage ideals. As luck would have it, a copy of the magazine was laying on a coffee table in a doctor's consultation room and was read by an editor of a leading newspaper in the big city of Cape Town. How the magazine got to that coffee table, no one will ever know, and yet that was the making of Jonathan Bale. The editor contacted Jonathan through the magazine, set up an interview, and within a short period, Jonathan was headlining the front pages of the newspaper with riveting articles in brilliant journalism.

It was not long before he became a household name and his attractive face spread across the advertising billboards.

Jonathan was handsome, and the camera loved him even without the use of photoshop. It was no wonder that he was headhunted by a TV channel that eventually changed his course of vocation. One network after another stood up and noticed this man that was making waves and increased the ratings no matter the show.

Along with his stride into fame came the A-listed lifestyle. A small one bedroom apartment was no longer good enough. A second-hand VW Golf was too unreliable, and it had to be traded in for a more modern, more expensive car. That in turn also became mundane - speed, style, and sporty replaced practicality.

He met and married a beautiful model (naturally) during this time of the high life, set up a home in a penthouse of a luxurious five-star apartment building. His son and daughter wanted for nothing, relishing the limelight holding daddy's hands while cameras flashed up the perfect, rich modern family. On all accounts, Jonathan had kept his image squeaky clean, the perfect doting family man, righteous, kind, generous, giving, never forgetting his roots; the all-around perfect human being.

When the announcement of a new show by the TV networks, and that Jonathan was to host it; the world went into a wild frenzy as the countdown to the pilot episode began. No one except those involved naturally knew the form or fashion of the expected show. A talk show yes; but what kind of talk show no one surmised. The public was exhausted by what they believed it would be.

And so, when Jonathan stood in the shadows of the studio, the lights were dimmed, the live studio audience (that had paid a fortune to sit in those seats) hushed with a good deal of difficulty. Everyone backstage held their breath; this was the moment. The start of the biggest thing on TV talk shows.

The music blared out the theme song, Jonathan walked to the center of the stage – the audience saw a movement and unable to contain their excitement any longer began to cheer – a single light hit the center of the set and Jonathan.

The perfect smile of the perfect host in his navy blue Armani pinstriped suit lifted his arms wide in welcome to all those watching all over the world. Minutes ticked passed before the audience calmed down enough for him to speak.

'How you doing?' he called out to the world.

It wasn't only in the audience that he got a resounding cheer of "Okay!" from; it was people in their seats in their homes, their places of work, restaurants and anywhere in the entire universe where this show was beginning its walk of fame.

'So thrilled you could join our exciting new show. It has sure been an exciting ride to here hasn't it.'

The audience, the world, yelled their replies.

'Okay, so are you all curious as to what this show is all about? Do you want to know?

He teased, baited, and tickled the audience until the microphone in his ear told him it was time. It was all about the timing. Get the audience to the point of hysteria then satisfy their curiosity because at this peak of enormous hype they'd buy anything.

'This show is going to be greater than any talk show ever in the history of TV; our guests will be leaders from all spectrums and from all over the world. We want to debate, argue, discuss and argue every angle of every topic imaginable. Among these worldly issues we will also look at different religions – now I'm sure those will be heated debates.

The audience for a second considered what was said and then burst out in a combined cheer of approval.

Now it is without a doubt that if any other host had announced this, it would have been received with animosity rather than enthusiasm.

Religion would become the new fad, the new fashion, the new issue of the world thanks be to the smooth-talking, convincing, lovable Jonathan Bale.

Just before he ended the pilot show, he held a carrot out for all to catch, 'After a few episodes, we will be announcing some super exciting news that will make every person sitting in these seats ecstatically happy. So get those tickets you never know if it will be your turn. Thank you all for watching our very first episode of "The Bale Show." Take care and goodnight."

He bowed slowly and gentlemanly never ceasing to smile, straightened up slowly bringing his arms out wide in an embrace to the universe. He was the master of the networks. He was the master of the world. Everyone would listen to his every word and believe it. He was that first-class, and he knew it. He bowed again still smiling. The cameras faded, the audience exploded in rapture.

Every show for the entire season was sold out by the time he walked off the stage.

He walked into loud applause from every crew, staff, management, owners, and dignitary waiting in the wings. His back ached from the congratulatory slaps he received as he made his way to his dressing room where a bottle of the best Champagne, flowers, chocolates, and caviar waited.

Cassia, Willow, and Zayn Bale eagerly and proudly welcomed their husband and father in the privacy of his dressing room.

'We are so proud of you darling. You did a most fantastic job out there. I love you. So proud of you.' Cassia, swelling with pride, kissed and hugged Jonathan.

'Daddy, the people clapped so much.' Willow said hugging her father's legs filled with pride.

Zayn in his father's arms hugged him around his neck tightly, not exactly aware of the enormity of the occasion at only two years old.

Jonathan released his family and sat in a chair breathing heavily. His elbows rested on his knees while he rubbed his face in his hands smearing his stage makeup. He looked at his little family beaming with love and adoration 'We did it. It was a success.' He breathed out slowly.

'You did it. You were brilliant.' Cassia corrected him.

Jonathan glowed in the realization of his accomplishment.

Chapter Two

The celebrations of the pre-empted success of the show flowed over at the studio in high spirits. The celebratory champagne waited patiently on the melting ice until the rating results were released.

The wine flowed, and the beer guzzled as the party swung swiftly into momentum. Cassia and the children stayed close to Jonathan among his continued appraise and adoration. However every so often Jonathan was whisked away to chat with the main dignitaries and the like, and Cassia with her children sat like pretty wallflowers against a backdrop of intertwining vines.

'Can I have your attention, please? Please, people just for a second quiet down. Your attention please.' A man holding a few sheets of paper bellowed above the din of the party. He repeated himself several times and assisted by several people dishing out the same instructions.

A few minutes passed until finally a hum was hovering waiting for Mr. Eckenberg, the owner of Channel SA9, to speak. 'Ladies and gentleman, Jonathan,' he looked around for Jonathan and so did everyone else 'where is Jonathan? Someone find him he must be here for this.'

A few men disappeared into the hallways calling out his name. Cassia was slightly embarrassed when asked where he was. 'He left with a gentleman a few minutes ago.' She replied.

A few more minutes went by before Jonathan came rushing into the studio ushered by those that went looking for him. His face hot and flushed although, he was expert enough to recover quickly. 'Sorry about that people, had to find a moment to answer a call of nature.' He smiled, blushed and everyone laughed.

'Jonathan stand here by me my boy,' Mr. Eckenberg continued to stridently make his announcement 'I have with me the ratings for tonight's pilot episode of "The Bale Show." He paused for dramatic effect as the people called for him to stop teasing them. 'It's way outta here! Beaten any record that ever existed! We have a hit! We have a hit!' He held the papers in the air and cheered. Everyone went wild, raising their glasses, spilling the contents and cheering, hugging each other, shouting at each other in excitement and mostly everyone was trying to get Jonathan's attention to congratulate him.

If one did not know better, it could have been said that Jonathan had just won an Oscar for best performance.

Sometime after the announcement Cassia, with their children who were extremely tired by now, managed to get to speak to her husband. 'So proud of you, congratulations to all of you.'

'Oh, babe I'm so happy. Wow, can you believe those ratings? I hoped for good ones but what we got – WOW.' Jonathan was still hardly able to contain himself.

'I know you need and want to stay longer, but I must get the kids home, so I will see you much later I presume.'

'Are you sure?'

'Don't be silly. Of course, you must stay, this is your moment. I won't wait up. Love you and well done again.'

'Thanks, babe. Love you.'

Cassia left with the children and Jonathan was free to be adorned. It was easy to disappear now and then with someone that was willing to show their admiration for him in more ways than one. The alcohol flowed in abundance that no one knew who was coming or going in whichever direction.

By later that morning when Jonathan finally straggled into his bed, no one would remember half of what happened in the latter hours of the party and those that did kept mum.

When he floundered into the living room late the next morning, the sun shone so brightly he felt his head was going to explode and covered his eyes for protection. Cassia giggled and drew the blinds closed in sympathy toward him. He sat gingerly in his leather recliner groaning in agony. 'Never again.' He moaned clutching his stomach and his head at the same time.

'You not feeling well daddy?' Willow asked holding his hand.

'No baby girl. Not at all.'

'Willow, you and Zayn please play in your rooms. We can give daddy his celebration cake later tonight.'

'Oh babe, I'm sorry you made something special, and I ruined it.' He noticed through the squint slits of his eyes that they had redecorated the living room for a hero.

'It's okay, later is also fine. Drink this, and I'll have something for you to eat in a few minutes.'

Later that evening Jonathan was treated as if royalty by his devoted family. The Bale family had been escalated from the A-list to the A+ list if one even existed.

Show after show, the accolades rained down on the production, and in particular, Jonathan. The debates on religion, in particular, raged on as the media pounced on the discussion of each episode, creating more and more hype. Religion had never been so widely and openly prevalent across the universe as it was at this specific moment in time.

After five episodes, the big surprise was announced. The audience went berserk when they discovered they were the lucky ones to be filmed live during this announcement.

After a relatively calm first half of the show, Jonathan had revved the hype monitor up a few notches 'Who remembers the "big surprise we promised?'

'Here it is,' he added a dramatic pause, a smooth smile and crazed the audience, 'from this show onwards we will be giving every person in the audience a gift. We shall call it "Jonathan's most wanted things," this could be a simple voucher, or it could be as huge as a Porsche. But whatever the gift you will not go home empty-handed and nor will the gift be less than R50000.00.' He abated the audience with his charm; they were hysterical. Just then designer envelopes were dropped from the ceiling attached to a ribbon and floated in front of each person. 'Those envelopes are for you, but wait for my go-ahead to open them, and, by the way, this gift will never be revealed the same way in any show.'

Jonathan smoothed his showmanship smile, shining his white teeth enjoying the audience's eagerness to snatch and rip open the envelopes.

'Okay,' He paused dramatically 'Get them!' He shouted.

People scrambled to unhook the envelope from the ribbon. Some were standing, others stretching while there were a few that pulled the ribbon into them almost pulling the structure from the ceiling down. Then they settled back into their seats and waited for the go-ahead to open their envelopes.

Jonathan teased them for a second longer and then gestured with his hands 'Open.' The audience ripped and tore open the envelope, pulling out a card and screamed with sheer delight?

"Congratulations on your gift of a brand new Kia, sponsored by Masterson Kia, Cape Town." The news of this episode went internationally viral.

Chapter Three

Jonathan's personal assistant amid all the chaos of show resigned, claiming "personal reasons" of which she refused to disclose with anyone. Everyone at the studio was shocked as who wouldn't want to work for the most popular TV show in the world and even more so who wouldn't want to work with Jonathan Bale?

It was down to the last five interviews after hundreds of hopeful candidates. During the add break of the following show, an interview had been set up for Jonathan to attend. He did, after all, have the final say.

Linda Fulton, a beautiful woman of twenty-two years, with rich black hair and aqua blue eyes, porcelain skin and red lips – almost a mirror image of Snow White, arrived to watch the show while she waited for her interview. She sat in the guest living room and felt the intensity filtering through from the studio audience. She phoned her mother 'Mommy it's insane, you cannot believe the atmosphere here, it's incredible. And the studio is so huge it's so hard to describe, and there are so many people working here. I'm so nervous; I don't think I will get this job, I really don't. I think I might faint when Jonathan walks in the door.' Linda finally took a breath and stopped talking when her mother interrupted her non-stop sentence.

'Now Linda, just calm down, you cannot make Jonathan or the show bigger than you. Remember your faith. Remember you are a child of God and you must not let the world rule your decisions.'

'Oh I know mom, I know how much I need this job to get me out of my financial situation. I know it will be such an opportunity for me, but I also know I have to keep God first. We have prayed about this so often I know I will make the right decision. I think I am just letting the moment get to me. It is so high profile – you know?'

'I know dear. I will say a prayer for you now.'

"Thanks, mom, I'm going to say a prayer now too.' Linda ended the call and was about to say a prayer when the door opened.

She almost fainted when Jonathan Bale, the TV show icon, entered the room and was formally introduced to him. She looked at him; he was almost larger than life itself.

For a few seconds, she lost herself in his aura then checked back into reality and recollected herself. 'Hello Mr. Bale, it's a pleasure to meet you.' She extended her hand in greeting.

He took her hand in his firm handshake lingering before letting it go not taking his eyes off her. 'Please it's just Jonathan, and it's wonderful to meet you. Suzette, you can leave us now, I'd like to conduct the interview in private, please.' Suzette nodded warily and left closing the door behind her.

'Please sit Linda.' Jonathan motioned to her to sit on the couch and not the armchair.

Linda was completely awestruck and was having a raging battle with the enormity of the moment and her faith.

'Linda I must say your CV is most satisfactory, and I think you and I will work perfectly well together.'

'You've read my CV? Is there anything you want to ask or anything you need to know?'

Jonathan sighed and moved closer to Linda, never for one moment taking his eyes off of hers. He completely drew her into him as he milked her every urge to turn away.

'No, I think you're perfect.' He almost whispered without a trace of his lie.

'I am confident I will be efficient at the job and will not disappoint you.'

'Jonathan edged closer to Linda on the couch, he held her eyes in his 'Linda, you will never disappoint me I'm sure of it. The job is yours if you will just ..' He implored her still further with his eyes creeping nearer to her face 'just... you are so incredibly pretty.'

'Mr...Jonathan, what are you doing?' Linda was so intoxicated by the closeness of Jonathan and tried with all her might to resist him, to hang on to her high morals and pride.

'Don't fight this Linda; I knew this was meant to be the minute I laid eyes on you. The job is yours; we can be so good together. Please, Linda, I can't resist you.' His nose touched hers; his fresh breath flavored her lips. 'Please, Linda. I want you.'

'I can't Jonathan; I can't …this is so wrong. I have never..'

'Never what Linda?' He touched her lips with his – ever so softly. She groaned a little.

'I'm a virgin. I don't want to do this, please.' She tried futilely to stop his reaching arms wrapping around her waist, tugging her toward him.

'You want to Linda. I know you do.' Then he kissed her, opening her mouth to his. She tried to resist, but he held her tightly and continued to kiss her until she responded in kind.

'I'll be your first Linda and your last. I promise you.' He whispered into her ears as he caressed her neck until she squirmed wanting more but still trying to hold onto the last bit of her resisting will.

His hands moved all over her body; he whispered little nothings to her keeping her under his spell. He swooped her down until she was lying on the couch and he was on top of her 'Linda we must do this, it is right, please Linda.'

She moaned through his kisses and could resist no more and gave herself to him completely

Virgin she was no more!

Chapter Four

He sat up breathing heavily, immediately closing the buttons on his shirt, pulling a handkerchief from the pocket of his pants and cleaning himself. He closed his pants and stood up.

Linda lay on the couch in turmoil as the array of heated emotions rapidly wound down, and her common sense started to hit home. Tears drifted down her cheeks, increasing in time with her guilt and shame. She covered her face with her hands and cried, wanting so badly to be reassured by Jonathan and for him to comfort and hold her. Her clothes tangled in a creased mess about her; her blouse still unbuttoned exposing her naked chest. With one arm, she lamely closed up.

'Be at work at six o'clock tomorrow, don't be late.' Jonathan stood up, brushed his hair with his comb and left.

Linda was devastated and sobbed trying at the same time to re-dress herself. She hurriedly went to the en-suite bathroom of the guest living room and locked the door behind her.

'Oh, what have I done, oh no what did I do. How could I?' She hollered to herself in pain and utter anguish.

She sat on the seat of the toilet and rocked herself to and fro trying to squeeze out the disgust that was sweeping through her veins.

After a long and harrowing half an hour, she stood up and cleaned herself at the wash basin, but just looking at her body brought on the guilty act and was released through a welt of sobbing jerks.

Another hour and with someone knocking on the other side of the door, Linda washed her face, ran her fingers through her hair, opened the door and ran from the building, holding her breath, not looking at anyone on her way out. When she reached the fresh air on the sidewalk to the car park, she yelled out to the sky 'Nooo.' and leaned against a lamp pole, hugging onto to it for support.

A security officer, observing her extreme distress came to her aid, but she refused it. He would not budge and insisted he helped her to her car. Not wanting to draw any more attention to her evil and disgusting self she allowed him to lead her to her car.

Once inside and with legs that shook almost uncontrollably she slowly pulled away and at a speed similar to that of a snail she edged her way home.

'Thank you for joining us tonight, till next week take care and goodnight.' Jonathan bowed and reversed off the stage to rapturous applause.

'So how did the interview go? Do you have an assistant as of tomorrow?' Suzette asked with a vivid scowl on her face.

Jonathan returned her scowl with a dirty smirk of arrogance 'Yes I do. She will do just fine for me.'

'You're a pig.' Suzette spat at him.

'How about I fire you!'

'The graveyard is full of indispensable people you piece of filth.' Suzette stormed off to wrap up her work for the day.

Jonathan stared after her in puzzlement contemplating at her statement.

Linda dived onto her bed and curled into a ball, and cried, and cried, and cried for hours for her dirty indignity.

Drenched with her tears and weak; she slouched to the bathroom and began to run a hot bath in an attempt to wash the deed off her body. She knelt beside the bath and automatically began to pray 'Oh Lord, Oh please Lord I am in shame, I have sinned in the worst way Lord, please, please, please forgive me, Lord. I beg of you Lord; please forgive my weakness. In Jesus name please Lord, Amen.'

After so many tears had poured out of her soul, she still found more to shed.

Once she felt a smidgen refreshed and could no longer feel Jonathan on her skin, she drove to her church, the Church of Christ, three blocks away from her apartment, and prayed all the way that Minister Clyde would be in his office.

Standing at the door to Minister Clyde's office, Linda's limbs refused to co-operate and knock or take another step into the office. Minister Clyde sensing someone was behind him turned around and was shocked to see a phantom of the woman he knew as Linda.

'Linda! Good gravy! What has happened? Sit down before you faint.'

She poured out her soul to minister Clyde, taunted that she had ruined herself in such a cheap and dirty manner. Horrified that her faith and her will to do God's will had been so weak. She wanted rather to kill herself than have the reminder every second of every day of what a sinful and undeserving servant she was.

With a lot of consoling and comforting minister, Clyde had finally managed to bring Linda to a state of normality and to speak of how to move forward from that point. They would study together every day for the next two weeks and after that once a week until Minister Clyde was satisfied Linda was able to move on from this disastrous act.

Linda would completely and utterly give herself back to her Creator and her King, but to do that the first thing she did was make a phone call, 'Hello Suzette, it's Linda. I will not be taking the job.'

'Can I ask why?'

'I think you know. Goodbye.' When that call ended the first tiniest piece of string started to knit Linda's life back together.

Chapter Five

The ratings and the front page news of "The Bale Show" went up higher and higher with every show. Suzette had carefully screened the next bunch of candidates for Jonathan's assistant, and in the end, the situation got so desperate that the show director insisted Suzette appoint whomever she felt was the best candidate. Jonathan's new assistant was a forty-five-year-old battle ax, namely Gertrude, who did not tolerate him or his time of day. Jonathan threw a fit and a half at her appointment but could do nothing about it. His temper and tantrums increased as the days passed.

The countdown by the audience had commenced, Jonathan stood in the wings while the music theme blared away through all the speakers. "One" the audience screamed, and Jonathan walked to the center of the set as the lights brightened and focused on him.

Alex, a stage handler who had been working with this particular company for many years longer than Jonathan, accidentally caused one of the stage lights to fall. It missed Jonathan by millimeters just as he scooted to one side when the stagehands and crew yelled for him to get out of the way. He fell over a chair in the process landing in an unceremonious manner on the floor. The light crashed and sent shrapnel of glass and metal spraying everywhere.

The audience screeched in alarm then went dead silent in anticipation of Jonathan's recovery.

Staff and crew all simultaneously left their posts and ran to the fallen Jonathan. A stagehand had got to him first 'You okay?' he asked anxiously.

Someone moved the chair releasing Jonathan's leg that was beneath it. Jonathan took a minute to assess his surroundings and what had happened before rolling onto his knees and pushing himself up.

He stood up, straightening his suit and hair, looked about him and yelled 'Who the blank-blank-blank-blankety-blank did that?'

The audience gasped.

A cumulative of voices informed him that it had been an accident and that the guilty person was indeed Alex.

Jonathan swung about searching for Alex, who was by now a frozen statue, still standing by the camera frame and fearing what was going to come next.

Jonathan brushed past the crowded people, took two wide steps and stood directly in front of Alex's face, staring him down with angry contempt.

'You are bleep-bleep-bleepety-bleeped fired. Get out of here you blip-blip-blipped moron.'

The audience gasped.

The producer of the show rushed onto the set grabbing Jonathan's arm and scurried him off the set at the same time leaving instructions for someone to get Alex to a safe place off the set too.

The rest of the staff and crew, not knowing how to react in such a situation, mulled about in the shadows waiting for further instructions and replaying the event in their minds and with each other.

The audience slowly roused their voices as they too began to replay what had just occurred and to express their mortification of their idol's actions.

The start of the evening's show was forcibly delayed while they cleaned up the set and Jonathan cooled down in his dressing room. The topic for the evening coincidently was on language behavior and, in particular, blasphemy. It was a sticky start to the show, and Jonathan knew before the show ended he had to recover it somehow. The front page news was already a given, unfortunately.

During the interval break, Jonathan sought out Alex hoping he had not left the premises yet. He found him in the produces office disputing his termination.

'Sorry, I forgot your name.' Jonathan said to Alex as he entered.

'Easy to fire someone when you cannot remember their name.' Alex retorted.

'Look I'm sorry, I apologize for firing you in front of everyone in such a manner. I was shocked, and I overreacted. You are obviously not fired.' He put out his hand to Alex in a peace offering gesture. His face perfectly pulled into a remorseful pose.

Alex hesitantly stood and shook his hand 'Okay.' He said and left the office not exactly enthusiastic to face everyone. However, everyone seemed to be on his side.

The interval was over, and Jonathan walked to the center of the set, mockingly dodging the lights and cameras. The audience was too much in love with him to not forgive his little tantrum and immediately laughed at his antics.

He stood in front of the set right in front of the stage, put on his best "I'm Sorry" face and held out his hands to the audience and the cameras.

'So I behaved extremely badly earlier, and I apologize to everyone here, and across the world and especially to the children, please don't ever do what I did. That type of behavior is never the answer and to show you how much I deeply regret my actions' he looked to the wings of the stage and to the crew standing around the set until he found Alex, 'Alex, please come here. Please.' He held out his hand gesturing toward Alex.

Alex hesitated at first not wanting to be Jonathan's peace offering, but the audience began to chant "Alex, Alex, Alex, Alex." He had no choice but to oblige.

'Thank you Alex. Ladies and gentleman Alex is not fired. Alex, please forgive me?'

Alex nodded his head and sheepishly slithered back to his spot.

The audience cheered.

Show recovered.

The ratings for that evening's show broke the record that the first pilot episode had already broken.

Chapter Six

Jonathan rode the pristine elevator to his penthouse, mentally exhausted and frustrated from the events of the day. He opened the massive uniquely carved wooden door and stepped into his home of peace and love and tranquility. Willow and Zayn heard his entry and ran as they always did to welcome their father, their hero, home. He bent down and hugged them both a little longer and a little tighter than usual. Cassia came up behind the children wiping her hands on a dish towel well aware of what had taken place on set.

'Hey, babe, how you feeling?'

Jonathan looked at her questionably enquiring with his eyes as to whether she had watched the show or not. Cassia motioned with a nod of her head for him to join her in the kitchen. He stood up and followed her.

Entering the kitchen, the children ran back to the movie they were watching; Cassia handed Jonathan a glass of red wine. Jonathan took a gulp of wine, let out a long breath of air and a heavy sigh. He leaned against the counter with his rear and started the conversation 'So you saw my little theatrics.'

'Babe, what happened? You have never lost your temper like that ever. Is the pressure getting to you?' Cassia could hardly understand what had caused her perfect gentleman of a husband to react the way he did. She stroked his hair around his ear lovingly.

'I don't know what happened. It was like something snapped inside of me when I fell over the chair. I got such a fright when that light crashed right next to me. My heart was pounding so wildly; I had no control over what I was saying it all just flew out of my mouth. I felt so bad, and for the entire first half, all I thought about was if that performance was my last. I just had to make it right again for the show, for Alex, and everyone involved. I still don't think Alex has forgiven me.' He downed the rest of his wine and poured another glass, throwing down a swig before standing it on the countertop.

Cassia embraced her husband 'I will call Dr. Dravid tomorrow and get him to prescribe something for anxiety just for when you need it. Jonathan began to protest, but Cassia put her fingers on his lips and insisted - he was too tired to bother arguing.

Cassia ran a huge hot bath with essential oils and bubbles and assisted Jonathan into the bath to soak away the day, and ease the tension in his body. He rested back in the massive tub drifting into a solace of tranquility. There was a tap on the door 'Come in.'

Willow and Zayn quietly stepped closer to the bathtub to say good night.

Cassia handed Jonathan two white pills and a glass of water before ushering the children to bed.

Jonathan relished the silence and the warm water shriveling his skin in its soothing therapy. He looked about at his massive en-suite bathroom – gold taps and towel rails, grey marble tiles, black marble surface top around the gold wash basins, water jets in the bath to massage your body (that were currently on), and the shower was the size of an average middle-class bathroom. He smiled at his afforded luxury which helped him to recover further.

An hour later he thudded directly from the bath, onto his custom designed king sized bed, with satin sheets; and thanks to the two white pills he fell asleep immediately.

His conscious however had other plans than allowing a peaceful night's sleep; he tossed and turned restlessly until at almost three in the morning when he was wide awake. He tried to go back to sleep, but to no avail, so he did the next best thing and went to the kitchen for a cup of coffee. While he had the chance of being alone and without distraction, he could catch up on some work. He had meant to research new material for the show.

The light flicked on and brightly reflected off the stone black marble worktops; the grey cupboards enhanced the black. Cassia never went to bed unless her massive kitchen was spotlessly clean. The grey tiled floor sparkled it was so clean that it could reflect your image. The water in the kettle boiled on the Smeg gas stove; the kettle whistled for attention.

Jonathan pulled out his favorite coffee mug – "World's greatest dad" was painted on it – and made himself a cup of expensive Colombian coffee. When he had these mornings of no sleep, he preferred the very expensive imported Colombian coffee to that of the Italian coffee brewed in an overpriced coffee machine.

He took his coffee to his home office, turned on his laptop and started researching. He had a niggle bugging his sub-conscious of something he could not yet figure out.

Chapter Seven

The advantage of living in such a high effluent and luxurious apartment building was that the Bale family had protection from the fanatical media. Not so in the public arena.

Jonathan pulled into the parking lot of the church he and his family attended and simultaneously was assaulted by a mass of journalist clambering onto his car, running with it until he brought it to a stop in a parking bay. The family usually adored the journalist's attention, but not today for obvious reasons.

People that had already arrived for the morning service helped to get Jonathan and his family into the building, fighting and pushing away the cameras that were callously shoved into their faces.

The Bale family slightly traumatized sat in their regular seats waiting for the church service to begin while their friends and other members comforted them, especially the children.

The journalists crowded the back of the auditorium, their cameras set up waiting, hoping for a scoop.

Jonathan, knowing that the scandal-starved journalists would not leave, got up and went to the back of the stage to speak with the pastor of the church.

The cameras went frantic.

He returned to his seat and spoke earnestly in Cassia's ear.

The cameras went frantic.

The pastor stood in front of the auditorium behind his pulpit. He raised his hands toward the journalists 'Before we begin service today; I have an announcement. Since we have been overrun this morning by these journalists, Jonathan Bale will give a statement to them. And then I asked you all please to put away your cameras and enjoy the rest of the service.' The journalists murmured and grinned in sensational hunger, nodding their approval to the pastor. The people seated in their pews had all turned around to look at the journalists and then swung back around again to face the pastor.

It was moments later when Jonathan stood up to a loud clicking of camera shutters, people's low-toned voices, and applause.

What the applause was for no one knew, but some felt it was justified.

He stood behind the pulpit without shame or anxiety - this was his talent; he played with an audience every week it was only the setting that was different.

'Pastor Mike, members of the congregation, press, thank you for affording me this opportunity to repent and to hear my apologies. Yesterday I behaved wickedly. I am ashamed of the way I reacted to the incident; I can only pray that Alex will truly forgive me and so will you all. That includes those of you watching on the TV. I cannot make an excuse for why I reacted the way I did. I simply don't have one, when I realized what I was saying it was obviously too late. Clearly, this is not a behavior we are trying to instill in our children and the future generation. So I beg of you, please, do not use that outburst as true guidance but to rather listen to my apology and learn from my experience. I ask God to please forgive me. Please forgive the harm I have caused, and I ask God that people will not do as I did ever in their life.

May I also ask the journalist to now, please turn off your cameras and remain for the rest of the service?'

His words were so sugar coated they melted in his mouth; he even shed a few tears that crawled into everyone's sympathetic hearts. Meekly he sat down next to Cassia after embracing Pastor Mike in a sobering hug. Cassia linked her arm through his and rested her head, crying, into his neck with such affection every person watching felt the tears she shed with their own.

The journalist switched off their cameras and left the building – the front page scoop was all that interested them, certainly not meaningless words from a pastor.

After the service Jonathan suggested they take a drive out to the country, to get away from the madness for awhile. Eagerly Cassia agreed, it would do them all good to have a change of scenery.

He drove their Mercedes S-class sedan out of the city, and immediately the stillness of the outer city limits relinquished the tension in the interior of the car. Willow and Zayn started watching a movie on their TV screens with the earphones on. Jonathan and Cassia sat in silence for several kilometers.

Way into their journey through the countryside Cassia broke the silence 'Any idea where we are going?'

Jonathan shrugged his shoulders 'Let's just see where we land up. It's been a long time since we've even ventured outside of the city.'

They smiled at each other Jonathan reached out to hold Cassia's hand that she'd willingly offered.

After an hour and a half of driving through luscious green forests and farmlands, hardly speaking but rather listening to their favorite music played just loud enough for them to hear and appreciate, Jonathan ushered his family into a country hotel on the outskirts of Ceres.

While Jonathan reserved a table for him and his family for lunch in the posh A-La-Carte restaurant, Cassia took the children to the bathroom.

'Uhm, Mr. Bale, so that wouldn't be the TV Mr. Bale now would it?' The concierge asked with a glimmer of hope and adoration in her eyes.

'If I say yes, you will not call the press I hope. Sure had enough of them this week.' He smiled his charming grin, flashing his perfect white expensive teeth.

'Only if I can have a photo with you, I love your shows.' She flirted.

'Okay, that we can arrange. You have a camera or phone.'

She whipped out her cell phone got to the camera app in a flash and stood next to Jonathan, her arm around his waist smiling in the pose for a selfie. Jonathan put his arm around her waist; his hand touched the front of her tummy as her waist was so tiny. As he bent down to her side to fit in the photo, her perfume whiffed up his nostrils. Immediately he was aroused.

'So you going to send me the photo?' He asked watching her delight as she excitedly checked that the photo was perfect. It undoubtedly was her next Facebook profile picture within the next few seconds.

'Really?' she asked surprised.

'Yes sure, here is my number.'

'Myra could hardly believe her luck – having a photo with the famous and gorgeous Jonathan Bale and getting his phone number too.

Cassia rejoined them with the children, and they were ushered to their table on the patio overlooking the vast vineyards and majestic mountains.

'This is our most private table only offered to honored guests.' She proudly stated with the warmth of a professional host.

'And we are most honored. Thank you.' Jonathan replied in slick response.

They weren't seated for long when his phone buzzed. 'I thought you were going to switch it off today?' Cassia asked a little disappointed.

'I am.' He pretended to switch it off. Instead, he only turned down the volume and observed as his beautiful model of a wife immediately released the frown creasing her emerald green eyes. He looked at her, leaned over and kissed her ever so tenderly 'I love you.' He whispered, stroking the back of his forefinger down her porcelain cheek.

She glowed, her cheeks red, and with the slight breeze, her jet black hair fluttered about making her more beautiful, more vulnerable than he had noticed in a long time. Already aroused by Myra's tiny waist he had the urge to grab her in an embrace and kiss the life out of her. He sat back and smiled, blowing her a kiss and chasing down the desires he was experiencing.

A waitress brought their drinks they had ordered and informed them the first course was on its way.

After the second course of the menu, Jonathan excused himself to go to the bathroom passing the concierge along the way, smiling and winking at her watching as her heart floundered into a crimson respondent.

Once in the bathroom stall, he locked the door and sat on the toilet (the lid down) taking out his cell phone.

He replied to her message "Thank you for the photo. You are beautiful."

He sat waiting just in case she sent a reply.

He kept the phone on silent, just in case, and watched the screen for a few minutes. It flashed alive; quickly he opened the message.

It read "Thank you. I am flattered, especially coming from you. I think you are a wonderful person."

He replied, "How wonderful?"

He waited, his heart beating slightly faster while his desire to conquer his urges took precedent in his mind.

"Where are you?" She replied.

"In the men's room."

The door flung open and locked shut. Jonathan smugly grinned. He prided himself on his charm. He clicked open the stall door, reached out and pulled Myra into his arms locking the door behind him again.

He left first leaving Myra to make sure she did not get caught leaving. She quickly locked the door, so she was able to adjust herself before another male came bursting through the doors. She looked at herself in the mirror, flushed and out of breath. She smiled at herself completely convinced she had won the heart of Jonathan Bale.

'What took you so long?' Asked Cassia when he finally sat down to begin the next course on the menu.

'I had the worst cramps, probably just the stress of the day.' He looked away and paid attention to Willow and Zayn instead.

'Is everything to your satisfaction?' Myra asked as she approached the table, gleefully gazing at Jonathan.

'Just fine.' Cassia said and without missing the star-struck look on Myra's face.

Myra hesitantly left them alone disappointed it was not Jonathan that had spoken to her, that he had other than a nod and a smile ignored her.

'Shame she can't believe she is in your presence.' Cassia giggled.

'What do you mean by that?' Jonathan retorted.

'Oh come on babe. All women glow when they're in your presence. We all know that.' She laughed teasing him.

'Do you glow?' He teased her back placing his hand on her thigh under the table sliding it up to her groin.

'Stop it.' She laughed pushing his hand down. 'Wait till we get home.'

'Don't know if I can wait that long.' He kissed her intently until the children groaned their disgust and he pulled away laughing.

He leaned backward in his seat looking over his shoulder behind him, deliberately wanting to see Myra as she stood sullenly watching them in the shadows.

The meal finished, and while Jonathan paid the bill, Cassia walked on the smooth, bright green grass in front of the patio. He felt the vibration of his phone in his pocket took it out half under the table and read the message. "You are incredible. Can we meet again soon?"

Jonathan replied, "Who is this?"

Myra was devastated finally realizing that she had fallen victim by the world's smoothest player, that all she had done was to increase his desire to have his wife in fullness and that she was wrung out like a used wash rag. She ran out of the building to her car not wanting to see him again.

He was beyond happy all the way home. The children went straight to bed tired from the traveling, and that meant Jonathan could ravish Cassia until his frustration, desires, and needs finally met his lust.

Chapter Eight

The sun was yet to rise as Jonathan drove out of the basement parking garage of the building. He was as calm as the quietness of the morning – rush hour was still three hours away. He slid his slick sports car onto the road and pushed down hard on the gas pedal. The car revved into speed, and soon Jonathan and his baby were hightailing down the highway - way, way over the speed limit towards the studios. He loved this time of the morning when he was able to get a little power out of the engines and drive the car as it was meant to – super fast. If he did ever get caught well then he was Jonathan Bale after all, and he was positive he would get away with it, or he'd just pay the fine. It definitely wouldn't make a dent in his bank account. He breezed into the studios whistling, smiling and greeting everyone, even if it was just a nod of his head.

'Jonathan.' Glynn shouted from his producer's office as Jonathan was walking past. He stopped in his tracks, backed up about four paces and popped his head in Glynn's office door.

'What's up?'

'Come in. Close the door.'

Jonathan proceeded to do as instructed not losing his bounce since he had woken up.

'There a problem?'

'Have you seen the headlines this morning?' Glynn asked and handed a copy of the Times newspaper to him over the desk.

Jonathan sat in the chair and opened the paper to see the huge photo on the front page of himself behind the podium of his church "Bale gets bailed out." the headline read. He read the article to the end gave a "humph" afterward and handed the paper back to Glynn.

'And?' Jonathan asked not sure whether they were happy or unhappy with the article.

'Bravo!' Glynn applauded. 'We couldn't have scripted that better ourselves. Mr. Eckenberg phoned and told me to congratulate you on the excellent damage control.'

Jonathan laughed, lifted his hands from the arms of the chair and said 'What can I say, it is my gift.' He was smug and full of it, and he knew it. He knew he was taking the credit as if he had planned the whole thing, but who would know otherwise unless he informed them, so for now, he would be the hero to the network bosses.

'One more thing, the gifts lately have been mediocre so in next week's show it is going to be a whopper, get prepared!

He saluted Glynn as he stood up and left the office whistling once more on his way to his dressing room.

He mirrored his image and was pleased with himself. He looked exceptionally handsome today. His sleek black suit enhanced his grayish blue eyes – a most unusual color that merely added to the intrigue of his personality. His thick finely styled hair matched that of the suit, perfectly groomed; the groomed gentleman.

A knock on the door interrupted his admiring thoughts of himself; 'Come in.' he said and groaned when Gertrude's face appeared around the door.

'Good morning boss.'

'Glad you know it?'

'Know what boss?'

'That I'm your boss. I can also get you fired too.'

'That's why I call you boss.' She mocked him. As much as he tried to get her to do or say something wrong he just couldn't. She had won every round of their continuous dance. 'You can't, you won't, so I wish you would give up trying.'

She went to his dresser table and plopped the script for the show on it. 'Well done on the damage control. It's the talk of the studio this morning.'

A little taken aback by hearing a compliment from Gertrude, Jonathan nodded his head never taking his eyes off her in distrust. 'Thanks, it's what I do best.'

'Really now. Hmm.' Gertrude replied on her way out leaving Jonathan's good mood dampened.

'No ways! She is not going to ruin my good mood today. She can go to hell; she is not going to win this round.' He spoke to himself in the mirror, reassuring himself that he was going to remain in his current mood status the entire day.

The pre-rehearsal meeting was announced to begin any minute, and everyone concerned sat around the large oval-shaped mahogany table in the boardroom.

Again Jonathan was praised for his supposedly self thought-up damage control article in the press, and again he took all credit for it. Everyone except Gertrude and Suzanne applauded. Jonathan stood and took a bow.

Chapter Nine

As Jonathan stepped out of the backstage door onto the street, his usual hoards of fans cheered at him in appreciation of another fine performance. Another successful show that debated religion; it was furiously argued and resulted without consensus.

The limo door opened, and he gave a final wave goodbye to his fans before climbing in. His status in the world had reached such magnitude it was no longer possible for him to drive his beloved sports car to work every day. Being chauffeured in a limo was also advantageous as he was constantly on the phone, tablet or his laptop.

'Home?' Mervin, Jonathan's personal driver, asked as he pulled the long body of the car out into the open street.

'Yes.' Jonathan closed the window between the two of them as soon as he had replied.

It was one of those evenings when you'd catch every traffic light red, and so the journey home was arduous and annoying. At almost every traffic light whoever pulled up next to the limo would hoot and wave hoping Jonathan would wind his window down and greet them. Mostly he didn't, but they would yell and shout out to him and then have the pleasure of telling all their friends and family they parked next to his limo. A highly insignificant and pointless exercise on their part and yet they felt elated by it.

Jonathan had just put his phone down on the wide seat; he reached to the bar cabinet when he felt a strange presence around him. He looked about and obviously not seeing anything or anyone shook his head and resumed his act of opening the cabinet door.

He leaned back and shook off his suit jacket, folding it neatly and placing it tidily alongside the cell phone on the seat. Shifting in his seat slightly forward, he opened the whiskey decanter, savoring the aroma, and filled the glass three-quarters fill.

The same strange sensation whirred about him again, and while leaning back into the seat, he looked about him again ready to chastise himself once more.

Instead, he jumped into the corner of the seat when he noticed a man sitting next to him.

'How? Where? How? Who are? How?' Jonathan rambled; his hands shook with fear and fright spilling his ludicrously expensive whiskey all over his designer pants and the seat. He tried to take a sip to calm himself, but that only landed up being spluttered over his immaculate shirt and tie. He somehow managed to put the glass that contained a few drops left by now, onto the shelf the cabinet door provided.

In fear and panic, he pressed the intercom to Mervin. It was disconnected.

Jonathan stared at the dark shadow of a person sitting next to him, his suit jacket untouched. He opened his mouth, but no words came from his lips. He tried again. Silence! His voice was gone.

'Jonathan, I am not going to hurt you.' A deep baritone voice rumbled.

With eyes wild and largely rounded, Jonathan stared at the shadowy form. A sudden thought struck him, and he pounced onto the window separating him and Mervin.

Mervin never moved a muscle, concentrating on the road ahead without acknowledging Jonathan's banging on the window immediately behind his head.

Jonathan flung himself back into the corner of the seat gripping the door with force, trying to open it.

'Jonathan, be calm. I am not going to hurt you.' The voice shuddered in his eardrums.

"How was it possible that this person got into the limo? How was it possible that Mervin had not heard or noticed anything amiss back here?" He scrambled his confused thoughts.

'Do not concern yourself with all the irrelevant questions Jonathan. I am here in your wonderful posh car, and I have something to tell you.'

Jonathan's throat was quivering as he tried to speak.

'You cannot speak for now. It is better this way.'

Jonathan's eyes were wildly wide with anxiety; they began to tear rapidly. His chest started to heave as he battled to correct his breathing and to get air back into his lungs after shutting them down in fright. Cold sweat seeped out of the pores of his skin, and inside he was whimpering like a dog begging for mercy.

'I can see that whatever I tell you now will not sit with you. I will visit you another time. Just remember only you can see me and while I am in your presence the world around you will not notice anything different about you. In fact, they will not even be aware of the minutes that have elapsed. Let's just say they will be in a limbo state.'

Jonathan did not nod, shake his head or acknowledge what the shadow had said – he only stared with crazy wild eyes.

'Okay, Jonathan I will leave now. You won't see me leave, and this will be like a nagging headache for you. You won't remember it, but your subconscious will have an itchy feeling that something happened. Like when you know you have to do something, but you just can't remember. ' The shadow laughed boisterously 'It won't help to tell or even try to discuss this with anyone as they will probably think you are mad or overstressed.' He laughed again louder. Jonathan looked to Mervin hoping he had heard this overly loud horrendous laugh but nothing – he simply continued to drive home.

When Jonathan took his eyes off Mervin, there was a sound peace in the car. He looked at his suit jacket folded neatly untouched next to him. That is all that was there with him in the car. He coughed returning his voice. He was confused and did not know why. He wiped his brow with his silk handkerchief wondering why he felt so bewildered and so anxious, why he was sweating for no reason and for goodness sake why had he spilled his whiskey all over himself and the car. He poured another drink, swallowed it in one mouthful poured another and sat back chasing down his beating heart. He sipped slowly on the whiskey pondering what it was he had to do that he was forgetting.

Mervin parked the limo in the private parking of the building and waited until Jonathan's bodyguards were in position before opening the rear door.

'Sorry sir, did I go over a bump to hard. You seemed to have spilled on your shirt. Next time sir bang on the window or yell at me over the intercom so I can be aware if your trip is unpleasant. Again I apologize sir.'

Jonathan grunted and walked toward the elevator. He had no rebuttal as he had no recollection of when it happened.

'What happened to you?' Cassia asked as he walked into the penthouse apartment.

'Mervin went over a bump a little too hard.' Jonathan shook his head. To Cassia, it was a head shake in disgust to Jonathan it meant confusion.

He took a long, long shower trying to wash away the nagging feeling in his brain and after eating a perfectly cooked meal and spending a few quality minutes with his children before they went to sleep; he sat in his favorite recliner watching the television news channels. Cassia brought him a glass of his favorite red wine and sat in the recliner next to his.

'Is there something I have to do or go to?'

'Pardon?' Cassia replied slightly bemused.

'I keep having this feeling that I've forgotten something important. It's very annoying.'

'Well, not that I know. You had better check with Gertrude. Send her a message now in case there is an important issue early tomorrow you have forgotten.'

Without replying Jonathan picked up his phone from the table next to him and sent Gertrude a message "Anything important on for tomorrow? Don't want to have forgotten anything.'

He waited, sipped his wine in fast gulps while he did so and held the phone in his hand.

His phone blipped, and quickly he put his glass down to retrieve the message.

"Nothing that is not on your planner, on your phone or tablet."

He immediately checked his planner. Everything on his planner for the next day was as he recalled. He gulped down the rest of the wine.

'Find out what it is?' Cassia enquired very curiously. She'd never seen him so concerned over forgetting something he wasn't sure he'd even forgotten.

'Nope, there isn't anything.'

'I think you just need a good night rest babe.'

'Perhaps you're right. I'll take one of those pills your doctor gave me.' He got up from his recliner and walked into the kitchen rubbing his head wearily.

With the last sip of wine, he swallowed the little pill, trudged wearily to his bedroom to hopefully overcome his weird thoughts and sensations of the evening.

He slept like a log until almost three in the morning, an hour before his alarm was to go off. He knew he wouldn't go back to sleep, so he slopped his way to the kitchen for a cup of his favorite Colombian coffee and then to his study.

He sat at his desk reading the emails that had overflowed his inbox. He yawned and turned around in his swivel chair to face the window and the shadows over the city. For a few minutes, he gazed blankly out into nowhere then he rubbed his eyes and turned back around to face his desk and his laptop.

He bolted right out of the chair when he saw a shadow of a person standing in front of his desk.

Chapter Ten

'I wonder if you are ready for me now Jonathan.' A deep voice echoed throughout his study.

Jonathan coughed and coughed trying to force his voice to work; it only resulted in a sore throat.

'If you remember last night in your car nod your head.'

Jonathan nodded feverishly.

'Ah good! You will only recall this when I am in your presence. Now I wonder if you are ready to hear me yet.' He held out what seemed to Jonathan as a hand, and a terrified Jonathan pushed himself backward into his chair tipping it over along with himself.

After a scramble and a scurry, he found his feet and stood up planting his back against the window. The hair on his neck stood on edge.

'I guess not. Well, I will just have to come again. You will be ready for me the next time. I will be sure of that.'

Jonathan coughed as he stroked his sore throat. He rubbed his forehead, wiping the cold droplets onto his hand. He frowned looking at his hand and touching his sore throat with the other hand.

"I must be getting sick. Better get something for this immediately. Can't afford to be sick now or ever." He thought while he dug in the medicine chest for suitable medication.

After taking two pills he went back to bed, Cassia was sound asleep beautifully dreaming, and so he calmly lay down next to her, closing his eyes hoping sleep would come to him swiftly.

That lasted about half an hour until he was wide awake again. He was a morning person, used to having to be up at the crack of dawn either at the studio or in his study. Naturally, he assumed this was the reason. His body and mind were not geared to be sleeping late in the mornings.

Finally, he researched and typed away on his laptop until it was time to get ready for another day at the studio. He had not felt that nagging feeling for the last few hours and felt highly relieved. After he showered, shaved and groomed, he admired his appearance in the full-length mirror.

The weirdness of the last few hours did not reflect. He was his normal self again. He smiled at himself, ran his fingers through his hair, pulled at the length of his sleeves and straightened up once more. To his reflection, he said 'You own the cameras, they love you, and the people love you. You are the greatest host ever. Make them love you, even more, today.' He winked at himself and left for work.

Gertrude tapped on his studio room door and entered 'Good morning boss.' It was her usual greeting said by way of acknowledging that she had seen him and not out of any manner of concern or respect.

He replied likewise 'Morning.'

She put his file on the desk with the days' program and had highlighted any changes from the previous day's mock-up program.

'Gertrude.' Jonathan called out to her as she was leaving the room 'You got a minute?'

She hesitated unsure as to the sudden gentleness in his tone. A tone of voice he had never used with her before.

'What's up?' Gertrude stopped and turned around. He was looking at her enquiringly – wanting her to hear him out -this was most unusual. It unnerved her.

'Do you ever have that feeling that you should be doing something, or you should have done something, but you just cannot remember where or what it is?'

'Everyone has that.'

'I know, but this is different. It's been for a few days now, and it's almost becoming an obsession. This morning I felt it was over, but once I was here, it started all over again.'

'Probably just the stress and madness of this industry, I'm sure this kind of thing has happened to every person involved in TV in one way or another. Take a pill.'

'I have. Yes, you probably right. Thanks, Gertrude, well let's get the day started then.' He rose from his chair and took his jacket off the coat stand. Gertrude had exited the room in a hurry before he decided to walk with her. The conversation they had just had was odd, and so out of character, any more of that and she would call the doctor for them both.

The lights on the set were dark, Jonathan stood in the wings of the stage as the audience cried for a change in status. One single spotlight shone an oblong shape in the middle of the floor; the audience yelled, the theme song chimed slowly building up to a crescendo until the nerves of the audience were at their tethers in exhilaration and then and only then Jonathan walked into the spotlight. All else dissipated and he shone.

He welcomed the world to his feet, introduced the guests and tickled their interests with what was to be the gift the audience would receive.

The nagging, uneasy feeling that plagued him had gone into the backside of his subconscious and Jonathan presented himself to the universe as the altogether, good looking, religious, perfect family man. He believed this to be the truth.

A few hitches here and there but none detectable by anyone other than the crew in the editing room. The end of the show and the lights went down; the audience disappointed that it was over mingled out of the studio while Jonathan swanked his way back to his studio room. He felt on top of the world relishing the comments from the people as he passed them. "Great show." "Fantastic show." "Awesome performance."

He sat smugly is his chair removing the makeup from his face watching himself in the mirror. 'Now that was a huge show. Huge.' He spoke to his mirrored image.

He fought his way into the large luxurious seats of the limo 'Home please Mervin.'

'Yes, sir. That was a brilliant show, sir.'

'Yes it was, wasn't it?' He switched off the intercom and poured himself a glass of whiskey – neat. He sighed as the flavor flowed down, enjoying the smoothness of the liquid slide down his throat that felt scratchy the last few days. He put his head against the backrest of the leather seat and shut his eyes. He was calm, relaxed and strangely eager to be at home with his wife and children.

'That was an amazing show babe.' Cassia said hugging her husband in a welcome home embrace.

The children too gave him the hugs he had subconsciously hungered to have. Instead of going to the kitchen for a glass of wine as he did every other night he went with the children to their living room and watched their DVD with them. He asked questions about the movie and the characters, teased them and tickled them - a moment so rare in this household of Bale. Cassia stood behind the couch watching in utter amusement as the love of her life played so affectionately with their offspring. It had been a long, long time since she could even remember him sharing anytime, except when in public, with Willow and Zayn.

Totally out of breath Jonathan escaped the clutches of the children and left them to finish the rest of the movie.

He joined Cassia in their living room and rested in his recliner sipping his wine. Cassia sat on his lap, sliding her arms around his neck and kissing him gently on the forehead 'Now where has this man been hiding in this body for so long?'

Jonathan chuckled, placed his fingers on her hips exactly on the spot he knew she was exceptionally ticklish and squeezed 'Hmm, I think he is here.'

Cassia squealed laughing trying to wriggle out of his grip. Their laughter and giggles attracted Willow and Zayn, which were unable to resist the temptation not to join in. It was a free for all - four bodies running around a plush penthouse apartment, in designer clothes on lavish flooring having a natural way of life.

They collapsed on the floor in the middle of the living room heaving in exuberated cheerfulness. Jonathan pulled them all up into his arms and held his family to his chest as a doting, loving father would do on any given day.

Willow and Zayn went to bed sure of pleasant dreams filled with laughter and the sunshine. Jonathan and Cassia shared an evening of such intense intimacy which was only ever equaled to when they were on their honeymoon.

As usual, Jonathan was awake in the wee hours of the morning while his family slept soundly. He looked at the clock as got his cup out of the cupboard for his usual cup of coffee and took out a rusk to munch on – one o'clock, much earlier than usual. He yawned, waiting for the water in the kettle to boil, tapping on the countertop hurrying it up.

With the cup in his hand and another rusk in the other, he turned to start his day in the study.

As he turned the shadow stood before him – It jolted Jonathan into such a shock that he released his hold on the cup and sent it crashing. His favorite and also the only cup he used was shattered all over the kitchen floor.

Chapter Eleven

'How did you get in here?' He dashed for his phone on the counter - the shadow was faster, and it too lay in pieces on the floor.

'We cannot delay this any longer. I will tell you why I am here. Why I have chosen you, this time, you will remember what I have said, and you had better follow it verbatim.' He paused allowing the words to sink in.

'Who are you?' Jonathan stuttered.

'Patience; all will be revealed at the correct time. To the study!' A dark shadow resembling an arm pointed toward the study. Jonathan obeyed trembling.

'Please don't touch my family. I have money, anything, just don't hurt them.'

The shadow bellowed a large deep and forceful laugh. Jonathan was sure his family would awake to the sound and be captured by this shadow. He wanted to run, but he was frozen to the ground he stood on.

'There is nothing in this world you can give me that I cannot take for myself.' His presence was overwhelming, and Jonathan began to feel woozy 'Can I sit down.' He asked already holding onto the chair.

The shadow remained silent, and he took his chance to sit hoping it was not the wrong choice. He could not bear the sound of that laughter again it made his brain, and his inside want to explode.

'You will conduct an interview with me.'

'What?' Jonathan was perplexed. 'An interview? All this just for an interview?'

'There are of course stipulations which if not adhered to – well you can use your imagination as to what I will do to you and perhaps your family.'

Jonathan stiffened.

'I'll meet you on set at three o'clock. That gives you just over an hour to make sure there is no one present in the studio or anywhere near it. That includes the usual crew in the control rooms. It MUST be just you and me. All the cameras must be pre-set to run automatically. I believe you know how to do that.'

Jonathan nodded.

'The interview will run from three o'clock – not a minute later – to six o'clock and again not a minute later.'

'What then?' Jonathan hesitantly asked just in case he overstepped his mark.

'The editing staff, producer, and directors, you know, the ones in control, may enter at six fifteen. The show will go on air throughout the world at eleven o'clock. You need not worry as to how the world will know about it. They just will!'

Jonathan had no words, and when he focused his eyes again, the shadow was gone. It took him a few seconds to gather himself before he dashed to his room and changed into the first suit his hands touched.

Within minutes, he was speeding in his sports car toward the studio, this time without holding back on the power of the engine.

He arrived on the set fishing the security staff out with a lame excuse of needing privacy. They admired him so much it did not cross their minds to question his requests.

He phoned Gertrude, Suzanne, Mr. Eckenberg, the director and producer within minutes. They certainly did not appreciate the early phone call but got the gist of importance and urgency and agreed to be there on time.

He felt bare. It was the first time he sat in his chair without makeup, without his hair brushed, without the spotlight.

He waited. It was two fifty-nine.

The nerves on his back stood up when the shadow seated himself in the chair next to him.

'Everything set as I requested?'

'Yes.'

'Then we can begin.'

Jonathan shuffled in his seat; this was such an uncommon ground for him. He usually read from the teleprompter or instructed via his earpiece. He cleared his throat then spoke.

'Ladies and gentleman, this is a different show today. I have been requested to host this interview privately to which I have obviously agreed to do. I hope you will enjoy the show.'

He turned to the shadow that was now no longer a shadow but a grave-looking man with hard features and black, the darkest black imaginable, pair of eyes. He sat in the chair like a human and yet he looked to be afloat in the chair.

Jonathan shuddered with fright and lost his words as he stared in horror.

'Continue Jonathan.' The shadow instructed with a coarse gruff tone in his voice.

He cleared his throat and simultaneously coughed a few times very aware of the cold, clammy sweat that was piercing his skin. 'Who are you?' He finally asked still unable to shake the quivering inside of him.

The man replied 'I am Satan or as most like to call me; the devil, the accuser or fallen angel of God.'

Jonathan gasped and sucked in a gulp of air almost choking himself in the process.

Satan waited while Jonathan composed himself almost fully. 'What questions do I ask him? But can it really be him?' Jonathan's mind ran rampant as he fought to restrain the thoughts and concentrate.

'Satan.' His voice came out too high revealing his fear, he coughed again and spoke again, trying with all his might to keep his fears in control. 'You say you are Satan. Can you prove that you are?'

'I could tell of all your indiscretions, that poor girl Linda but that would not be fruitful, so let me do this.' He paused and with it an evil, terrifying grin smeared across his face.

'I asked you to make sure that no one was to be here, is that so?'

'Yes and I did.'

'No, you did not. Alex, do come on out from behind the wall in the back of the studio. I know you're there. You see Alex is one of my devoted followers, a Satanist at heart and worshipper of note. You humiliated him, and while you believed he forgave you, he has been plotting his revenge all this time. He never left the building last night but hid in a closet. Once he was alone, he began planting bombs around the studio with the plan of setting them off as soon as the show began today. Hence killing you, the staff, the audience and himself, is that not right Alex.' He turned his head eerily to where Alex had come out from behind the wall.

Alex took one look at Satan and started run for the exit.

Satan laughed that grotesque loud bellowing gaff and shot his hand out toward Alex.

Alex caught alight and fell writhing in pain and anguish, screaming until the flames overcame him and when he died he turned to black ash. Nothing around the burning body of Alex was affected, touched, melted or disturbed in any way. The black ash slowly disappeared into nothing.

Jonathan cowered into his seat crying for mercy, mortified at the sound of Alex's painful screams, terrified that he was next.

'I will not harm you - Yet!'

Jonathan wiped his face of the tears swallowing down his sobs, his heart hammering against his chest as the adrenaline flushed through his body. He took another few minutes to compose and recollect his thoughts, and his nerves that were by now shattered.

He continued in a croaky voice 'If Alex was one of your followers, why?' he paused to prevent the burst of sobs from escaping 'Why did you do that to him?'

Satan cracked another horrendous laugh 'Got your attention did it not. Anyway, he was going to land up that way in the end, so it made no difference.'

'Why do you want this interview, I am very confused.'

Satan exposed that evil grin of his and almost hypnotized Jonathan 'That explanation will come later. First, don't you want to know how I came to be?'

'Yes. Let's start with that. Will there be any more dramatics, please I couldn't handle it.'

'That depends on you, but for the moment there are no other people in the building, and I have secured all the locks. So we can continue.'

'Thank you.' Jonathan moved his body position once more to a more professional pose, thinking if he sat more correctly he would feel more like the interviewer and not his guest's puppet. 'Please explain how you came to be who you are?'

Chapter Twelve

Satan slithered into the seat, imitating man making himself more comfortable. A smirk creased his hardened face while he watched Jonathan watch him with great expectation.

'I will take you back to the beginning of time. God created all things; this is true. He created the angels to serve Him. I was one of them serving my Master in awe of His magnificence, and I was His personal entertainer, it was my job.'

God's glory shone so bright at times it was even difficult for us angels to look at Him.

I'm sure you can remember the story in the Bible of Moses and how his skin shone after being in the presence of God - I'll get to that later – but that is what it was like for me. After a long, long era exposed to God's radiance, I thought that I had absorbed some of it. And then after many more millions of years, don't forget now this was not your years, God's time is not the same as yours - I believed that I had the power of God. In my egotistical mind, I had not realized that the shine I had was minuscule compared to that of God's - a drop in the ocean.'

'I convinced a few other angles that we were equal to God in power – now that took some doing – but I convince them I did and we formed a rebellion against God.' Satan chuckled wickedly to himself at the memory of the event. He shook his head and with his long boney crooked fingers wiped his brow and continued. 'My comrade angels and I went to God and demanded that His throne be turned over to us.' Satan let out a grunted snort and shook his head again. 'Was He angry? Let me tell you this. This world and every inhabitant that has ever existed on it has not known the wrath of God as we did at that moment; God was so infuriated he created hell, Oh yes, hell is real. Very real and the way the Word describes it in the Bible, so it is; believe me, you don't want to go there.'

'This is funny,' Satan smiles widely exposing his disgusting teeth 'my followers, Satanist, they honestly believe that I control hell and that I will keep a cool place for them in hell.

What a joke.' Satan crashes out a roll of thunderous laughter that brings tears to Jonathan's eyes it hurts so much.

'Watch this.' Satan motions with his hand and an oval portal blended with the wildest colors of red and orange, with a black hollowed center forms between him and Jonathan. 'Look through that portal.'

Jonathan hesitates naturally untrusting and afraid.

'Do it!' Satan hollers.

Jonathan immediately obeys and cautiously edges his face into the portal that is floating in mid-air.

Jonathan opens his eyes to what will probably haunt him for the rest of his life. The flames are too intense for him to keep his face in the portal for very long. His eyes feel as though they have melted out of their sockets, his ears are burnt red. He is only just able to see what Satan has shown him.

He has seen his place in hell. It's a place of fiery heat that will consume him endlessly without easing without relief. Satan shows him how demons devour him each day and then spit him out to return and repeat the procedure over and over again. He watches himself in hell screaming in pain so excruciating; the gnashing of his teeth so audible it is unbearable.

He pulls his face from the portal in a panic and then throws up on the floor next to his chair. His heart is racing toward hysteria. He wants to run but instead flings himself into his chair gripping onto it, cowering for mercy from Satan. Satan is almost hysterical with his grotesque laughter.

Jonathan cannot speak he battles to control the mayhem welling up within him.

'How do we prevent that?' Jonathan trembled.

'I will get to that at the appropriate time. Now, where was I? Oh yes – hell. God's fury ignited a spark of hell and banished us to it. But God spared me unchained to the burning fires that gouged out the pit of your soul eternally. I must re-iterate, hell is a thousand more times worse than you have just seen.' Satan shuddered at the mere thought of it.' I will be going back there, and this time, there will be no release for me, there is nothing I can do about it, and I dread it like you will never understand.'

He covered his face with his grotesque hands causing Jonathan to almost vomit. He put his hands away, sighed and shook off the image that was haunting him. 'I think God spared me in the hope that I would change and repent, and then he would remove hell, but I was bitter and disappointed and yes I was angry, so I made hell my kingdom. I felt powerful reigning over those that were weak and powerless to do anything other than cry in pain and anguish. I always hoped that the love God had for me before I betrayed him was still valid, and he would forgive me. He did love me and, of course, the other angels that turned against him too but immensely hurt by my or our actions. God turned His back on us, so to speak, and we were left to dwell in those red flames.' He held his stomach, or rather an area of where it was meant to be and almost cried. 'Oh those flames, those flames. They never stop. Never!' His face distorted into a painfully stricken torment mixed with a hateful surge. Jonathan slowly moved back into his chair, his legs slightly trembling fearing another outburst or another view into that portal of hell.

Satan's face slowly eased, and he looked at Jonathan realizing he had frightened him. 'Sorry, did not mean to frighten you again, just yet anyhow, but you have to understand the seriousness of hell for me to continue this interview.'

'I do. I do.' Jonathan hastily said. Cold droplets hung on his forehead in fear, but at the same time Satan's word "just yet anyhow" spun through his mind, terrified enough as it was and yet this was still not what the extent of his fear was going to be. He shivered, motioned with his hand for Satan to carry on, not that Satan required him to do so.

Satan readied his position to speak but thought about his next words carefully, tapping his thighs with his hands hidden under the long sleeves of his cloak. 'So where were we? Oh yes! There we were all in hell, and then God decided to create the Universe and for whatever reason God pitied me and allowed me to roam around His universe under the condition that I did not derail any more of His angels. Naturally, I agreed. This is where all my fun and what I thought was to be my revenge began.'

Chapter Thirteen

Jonathan took a drink of his water. His eyes were bright and fearfully eager to hear what Satan was to say next, even if he was still apprehensive he enthusiastically wanted to hear more from Satan reveling in the fact that soon he might have all the answers. A thought crossed his mind that once he had all of the answers to every question he would be so powerful. He could rule the world. A cynical grin pierced the corners of his mouth.

Satan looked at him sternly obviously knowing what he was thinking. 'Careful there with those thoughts of yours.'

Jonathan shot him a wide-eyed glance, embarrassed to have been so exposed. He quickly told himself to be careful in future.

'You do that.' Satan commented, and Jonathan shook his head shaking out any thoughts.

Satan laughed at Jonathan's discomfort. 'God decided it was time to create a masterpiece – Earth. Watching Him create it was – well there are no words expressive enough to explain the magnitude of His brilliance fully. But before Earth, when He created light and made the planets move to establish day and night, even the angels in hell sighed in awe.' Satan smiled to himself and Jonathan could clearly see the awe across Satan's face.

'Then He created Heaven, the sun, moon, and stars. It was too spectacular. And of course, it was time for Him to fill the Earth with all creatures big and small and then, of course, the Garden of Eden. It was pure beauty and spectacular. Ah if you could only have seen that creation you would never have destroyed this planet. It was something to behold. Pure splendor it was.'

Jonathan sat fascinated by Satan's recollection of the creation of time. He relaxed as he listened with so much admiration just as Satan had.

'I presumed I would dwell among this creation for eternity and in time God would forgive me completely, and I would be re-joined with the other angels. Instead, God created man. His greatest masterpiece! When God picked up the dust from the earth, I presumed He was just creating another creature and instead there became a man. Can you imagine watching that? You could never conceive that concept. It was without a doubt the most marvelous thing I had ever seen.'

Satan sighed before he continued. 'God gave dominion over all living creatures and things to Adam and put him in the Garden of Eden. I watched in the background as Adam gave names to everything, my jealousy increased at every name. And then God created Eve from Adam's rib, can you even remotely identify with how that happened. I doubt it. While Adam slept (okay it was a very deep sleep God put him in), he took out his rib and from that rib created woman. Well, I heard that day the angels sing like never before. That is when my jealously compounded into revenge. It was not right for God to give all this power and authority to a creation that had hardly been with God for a few days. I was infuriated. The hatred burned in me until it consumed me. I had to find a way to destroy man and become God's favorite angel again.'

Jonathan opened his mouth to say something, but Satan glared at him indicating he did not want to be disturbed.

'I overheard God instructing Adam and Eve not to eat from the Trees of Life and Knowledge of good and evil. Just by the way, it was not an apple. Where man came up with that idea I cannot remember, but it was a fabulous tree so stunning and glorious, unlike all the others that were magnificent in their own right. I immediately struck up a plan to get them to disobey God.'

Satan scratched his head thinking about the turn of events, and it sounded like sandpaper against a rough wall. Jonathan shuddered Satan laughed.

'I hounded Adam to take a bite of the fruit. He would not budge, he was so obedient, and so I turned my plan onto Eve. She was much easier to convince, actually too easy. She ate of the fruit and then gave it to Adam to eat. They were under the impression just like the rest of us angels that if they ate the fruit, they would die immediately. Guess that joke was on us hey!'

Satan snickered; Jonathan just sat and stared at him blankly.

'When Adam saw that Eve did not die immediately he convinced himself that I was telling the truth. He ate of the fruit and then knowledge filled both Adam and Eve and the look on their faces when they realized they were standing naked in front of each other was hilarious. Boy did I laugh at them.' Satan burst out laughing in his loud, boisterous hallowing gruff cackle.

Jonathan closed his ears and his eyes.

Satan cleared his throat and resumed in his normal voice 'I made for the bushes while Adam and Eve found leaves to cover themselves, and I heard God wandering through the garden. I waited like a lion ready to pounce on her prey for when God discovered what had gone down. Of course, when Eve told Him, I was the one who tricked her God was furious. He was beyond furious and made me less than all creatures; man and animals.

I remember he said "Because thou hast done this, thou art cursed above all cattle, and above every beast of the field; upon thy belly shalt thou go, and dust shalt thou eat all the days of thy life: And I will put enmity between thee and the woman, and between thy seed and her seed; He shall bruise thy head, and thou shalt bruise His heel."

Satan remained silent for a few seconds, contemplating those words.

'In these words, I immediately formulated a plan to make God a liar. For if the Great I AM would be unable to send Jesus then God would be made out to be a liar. And if God lies, all existence has to come to an end; earth, hell, space, etc. would have to cease which would free me from eternal death and torment.

'I did not see that coming; boy I was not happy. God removed Adam and Eve from the Garden of Eden, and the result was that man would now eventually die of old age or disease. That was when I formulated my plan to corrupt the world. I used my sidekick angels to bring fornication, bestiality, witchcraft, homosexuality, idolatry and all other immoral and sadistic uses to remove mankind as far away from God's love as possible. God was sorry he had created man, I was sure I was winning.'

Chapter Fourteen

Jonathan dared to challenge Satan that anyone could attest to being Satan by merely quoting Genesis, but he very quickly remembered Alex. No mortal man had the power or trickery to do that. He decided against the challenge and preferred to let Satan continue. He took another sip of water.

'Do you know the story of Noah?'

'Of course!' Jonathan replied indignantly.

'The world was a mess, all thanks to me; evil dwelled in every household except the household of Noah. I was king of the world and mankind was my servant.' Satan raised his hideous arms in a triumphant gesture.

'I used all of my wits to try and infiltrate Noah's family and to make them turn from God. Nothing worked. He was such a faithful servant.'

'Sorry,' Jonathan interrupted 'Don't mean to interrupt; I just want to check the camera, stretch my legs a bit.' He said as he stood up and looked at Satan and hoped he was not going to zap him for being so bold.

'Do your thing.'

Jonathan quickly stretched his legs as he took long strides to the camera. He checked it over in a hurry and strode back to his chair sitting in it all at the same time.

'You comfortable?' Satan asked sarcastically.

Jonathan neither nodded nor moved.

'Good. I knew God wanted to destroy the people of the earth because they were so corrupt and evil; they were so rife with filth, no matter what I did to get Noah to break his faith in God he only grew stronger. You know God does have a sense of humor.' Satan smirked.

'He told Noah to build this Ark. Good grief it was a huge boat – by the by, do you know since the Ark, all the boats and ships are built on this basis. When God told Noah to build this Ark I was confused; I had never heard of such a thing, no-one or any angel had ever heard of such a thing. We did not even know what a boat was. It was a monstrous proportioned odd looking house. He was mocked by every person every day. People threw things at him as they mocked him. I was adamant that Noah was going to cave and come over to my side.'

Satan shook his head 'I tell you that was the biggest thing that had ever existed and besides the idea of it floating we had no idea what it was going to do. God told Noah that he was going to bring rain down onto the earth and destroy everything in it. Rain! What was rain? There had never been such a thing before.' Satan sounded almost exasperated.

'Noah took hundred and twenty years to build that ugly monstrosity. Would you be mocked for a hundred and twenty years, day in and day out? I admired his tenacity. Do you know the Ark was built by an amateur and the Titanic by professionals?' Satan laughed at his joke terrifying Jonathan's ears.

'Then one day this water dropped down from the sky. It was an odd thing; no one understood what was happening. At first, people laughed at this wonder, but when it started to fall in torrents, people scurried for the shelter of their homes. But therein lay a problem you see. Houses were not built to be sheltered from rain since it had never rained before and it was not long when the roofs of the houses began to cave in, and the level of the water rose from the ground. People panicked and ran about trying to salvage their possessions and to find shelter. Noah by now had all the required animals and his family in the Ark just as God had instructed him. Who was laughing now hey? Not me!'

Satan shook his head in disgust. 'Still, no one ever believed the water would rise as high as the boat was. But the rain kept pouring down and down and down; I felt sorry for these people. Every corner of the earth was wet and drenched. The level of water rose and rose, people drowned by the second and everyone tried to get into the Ark and begged, screamed or cried out to Noah to save them. It was awful.' Satan hung his head in shame.

'Then the ropes holding the Ark snapped and it began to sail. Then and only then did I understand God's plan. It was an incredible sight, this huge ship sailing afloat that water, what magnificence and ingenuity. I acknowledged defeat, and I was highly annoyed. I knew I believed, that if God had not done that my second attempt to destroy God's throne would have succeeded.'

Jonathan coughed and cleared his throat. 'So where is the Ark now?

'God told Noah to hide it once they hit dry land and they were all safely on the ground.'

Jonathan sighed disappointedly. His sudden hopes of bringing breaking news and the discovery of one of the most sought-after missing links vapourised.

Satan merely smirked at Jonathan.

Chapter Fifteen

'Excuse me I need a quick bathroom break.' Jonathan requested.

Satan nodded. Jonathan did not wait for a second confirmation and shot out of his chair cantering out of the studio and down the corridor to the men's toilets.

He just made it, and while relieving himself, he wondered if he dared to phone anyone to let them in on what was happening. An image of Alex and the portal of hell flashed to the forefront of his mind, and very quickly he thought he'd rather not.

Hurrying back to the studio set and settling in his chair he looked at Satan's amused expression 'What?'

'Oh nothing, I have always been fascinated at the complex and perfectly designed human body and especially the need to get rid of the excess.'

'Well be glad you never have to be bothered with it. I can be a nuisance most of the time.'

They enjoyed a chuckle together immediately easing Jonathan's tense shoulders.

'Let's see, the next man so faithful to God I had tried to destroy was, oh yes Abraham.' A low growl dissipated from Satan's throat. Immediately the relaxed tension erased Satan snarled as he reminisced 'I resented Abraham the most of all God's Holy men. It is through Abraham that God made His covenant. Do you remember learning about Abraham? Through Abraham, all people would be blessed?'

Jonathan thought a little then nodded slightly.

'His children will be like the sun and the stars. The lineage of Jesus comes from Abraham, so many generations for a King.' Satan sighed.

'When I heard God tell this to Abraham, I had to destroy him. I couldn't let God's plan succeed and produce a pure bloodline until His Son came to earth. I had to infiltrate His plans and destroy all of God's believers.' He paused to make sure he had Jonathan's attention.

'So I paid a little visit to Abraham and Sarah. They were so old already; I used their age as my weapon. I quietly whispered in their ears that they must surely realize they are too old to have children. Where would generations be born from them when they are already so old? And I also convinced them that surely if God wanted them to have children, he would've done so by now. How was it possible for a barren woman to have a child? It wasn't so hard to win them over with that argument. Then I persuaded Sarah to let her husband, Abraham, sleep with the Egyptian slave girl Hagar. I put all the words in her mouth and softened Abraham's heart to her plea. They fell like rocks for it.' Satan shook his head.

'So Hagar has this baby, Ishmael. God cannot break a promise you see; He does not lie, and so all my plans were for naught. All I got out of it was the lineage of the Muslim people through Ishmael.'

Jonathan sits and raises his hand like a schoolboy in class 'So this is where they their religion from?'

'Yes. Now on with the story! God fulfills his promise to Abraham and Sarah and blesses them with a baby. At her age, ninety years old, she has a baby! I never thought it would happen, in any case, so Isaac is born. What a man he was.'

'What did you do to him?'

'Oh I tried plenty, but I'm not going to dwell on him. I'd rather speak about his son Jacob's one son - Joseph. Oh man, what a great man he was. I admired very highly.'

'You admired him? You did not hate him?'

'Yes I hated him, with a passion at that, but I had to admire him too, he was that great a man.'

Chapter Sixteen

'Now Jacob loved his youngest son Joseph; I suppose that was a natural thing since he was the son of his wife. In those days if the wife could not conceive the wife would allow the husband to sleep with the maid so he could have heirs.' Satan just remained silent thinking for a few seconds before he went on 'Now Joseph was obedient and gentle and very much, unlike his brothers. So for me, it was easy to convince the brothers to do all kinds of awful things to Joseph. But Joseph just sucked it all up and forgave them every time.'

'Why didn't you give up on him then and turn on someone else?'

Satan shot a glare at Jonathan 'Because Joseph was to play an important part in God's plan, not the others. The others were already in my trap so what would have been the point? Focus man!'

Jonathan shivered.

'When Joseph became of age I made the brothers sell Joseph into slavery. Joseph was thrown into a pit.' Satan cackled with utter evil.

'That pit was vile. It was like a grave. Just think of being buried alive, well that pit was about the same. Bugs, insects and all things creepy crawling around endlessly. Joseph could scream for help but who would hear him, and he didn't even bother to do that. He just waited! He knew God was going to rescue him.'

Jonathan rubbed his arms feeling the creepy crawlies rushing over him.

'What I did not know was this was all God's plan to have Joseph captured and put into slavery. I was so blazing mad when I discovered that.' Satan slammed his hand down on the chair which made Jonathan leap in fright.

'Joseph then gets sent to Egypt and works as a slave to Potiphar the pharaoh. I had fun and games there; those Egyptians were so gullible and easy. The best fun was with Potiphar's wife. Watching her trying to coax Joseph into her bed was hilarious. She would've made a fantastic high-class hooker in today's world, she was brilliant, and I know for a fact that no man could resist her; except Joseph of course.' Satan growled.

Then he sighed a defeated sigh 'After many years of Joseph being the "perfect man"' Satan indicted the inverted commas in the air while being very sarcastic 'Joseph became ruler over all of Egypt, only answerable to Pharaoh and what does the man go and do? He brings all of his family to him to live with him. He forgives them for all they did wrong to him – wow, that was a bitter pill to swallow – and Jacob (Israel) and the twelve descendants flourished for over four hundred years, and there was nothing I could do to wreck that no matter how hard I tried. But I'd bide my time once more.'

'There had to eventually be a new Pharaoh and did I like this one. He was my servant; this was my chance to destroy the world of God's servants. He hated the Israelites just as I did. He made them slaves again to the Egyptians. He made them do incredibly tough physical work like building the pyramids. Do you have any, any idea how heavy those huge stones were that they had to carry to build those things? I tell you, you could never imagine something like that era or what it was like to be an Israelite. I reigned supreme in those days; I thought I had finally ridden the earth of God's dominance.' Satan's ugly fingers rubbed his forehead.

'Yeah right! God had a plan. He was setting me up for a lark alright. The pharaoh was getting so mad, as was I that these Israelites were not dying off as a nation but, in fact, growing stronger. So I encourage his thoughts to have all the sons born killed by the midwives. But of course, I should've thought it through better and had the Egyptian woman be the midwives; they would've obeyed. The Israelite midwives feared God more than they feared the Pharaoh, so they simply disobeyed him. He was not happy. I planted the scheme for the Egyptian woman to drown the newborn sons.' Satan laughed. 'That was fun to watch.'

Jonathan cringed into his chair. The notion of throwing up was not far off.

'But of course, God was one step ahead of me and what happened – Moses gets born, his mother hides him in the bulrushes and of all the women to find him, it had to be the kind and gentle daughter of Pharaoh. I couldn't catch a break to destroy Gods' plan for mankind completely.'

'Now when Moses grew up, he was a strong boy but also with a kind heart. He had a major flaw, though; he stuttered, and I thought well there was no ways God was planning on using this man to rescue his precious Israelites. I mean come on! A leader that stuttered, it was absurd. But you see God knew I would think this and I, of course, was not paying enough attention. I was too busy wrecking havoc anywhere I was able to.'

Jonathan reached for his glass of water and realized it was empty and poured more into it. Satan watched him impatiently.

'So I presume you know the story of Moses?' Jonathan nodded finishing his gulp of water.

'Yes, Moses the stutterer. He frees the Israelites from slavery after four hundred years. Those plagues sent to Pharaoh were phenomenal, spectacular and fearsome. You've seen movies depicting these plagues have you not?'

'Yes, a few.'

'Well let me tell you, with all the cinematography you have in the world, with the greatest technology possibly you will never grasp the magnitude and ferociousness of them. And the sea that parted, now that was nothing short of absolute brilliance. It is in fact too great to describe, the height and strength of those walls of water that held up to allow over four million people; men, woman, and children, plus all their belongings that included all their cattle and chickens and whatnot. I was in awe of such power but at the same time, it infuriated me so much I told Pharaoh to send his armies to the Israelites and to bring them back to Egypt. A lot that did hey! So the Israelites wandered through the wilderness on their way to the Promised Land of Canaan.'

Satan had taken a breath of imaginary air before he continued 'You know people are so fickle. They so easily forget the miracle that God did for them and the favor He brought them. Never mind the love He had for them. I was rampant stirring up all kinds of discord among them. They complained. Oh, my word did they complain and moan. It was superb. It was brilliant to sit back and watch how easily bitter they became. And every time God appeased them they came round – until the next time. Moses, the poor man, made one little mistake – the only time I managed to get to him – and he hit the rock in anger. It was entertaining! God did not think so. God showed Moses all the land, but he died on the mountain and wasn't allowed to enter the Promised Land. God made that generation wonder around the wilderness for forty years. I had pleasurable time there. But what I did not realize was that God was depleting that disobedient generation and that the new generation that was obedient to God's commands would enter Canaan. Silly me, right! So Aaron and Caleb take a whole nation into Canaan, and the fields are ready for harvesting, and it is glorious in its entire splendor. Oh yes, they flourished there for many years.'

Chapter Seventeen

Satan is about to speak again when Jonathan raises his hand. 'I need another bathroom break, please.'

'Another one? Go quickly.' Frustration fills Satan's face as Jonathan bolts for the bathroom.

He is back in seconds 'Can I continue?' Sarcasm slid off Satan's tongue. 'Naturally, over time, there are more cities established and of course with great thanks to me -anarchy. The people forged war upon one another, and every time God's people were victorious. God's people rose above all, and there were some fierce wars. I thoroughly enjoyed them. Over time, I made the people want a real king. I implanted in their minds that a king will help them to rule, and they would have stability and all that nonsense. Boy, they were so stupid! So they got their king. The first king was Saul; he was weak and had no backbone, so it was easy to corrupt him. Then came his son-in-law David. What a great man, he was revered by everyone, especially after the Goliath episode. Honestly, there was not a single person who believed he would slay Goliath but God knew, and he made a fool out of me. I had to get Him back for that if nothing else. When David stated that he wanted to build a temple to honor God, I had to do something, to weaken him. I was quickly diminishing any stronghold I had in the world. Then I created the greatest love story of all time by default. I enticed Bathsheba to wash on the roof of her dwelling. She was beautiful to behold. Truly beautiful and carefully I whispered in David's ears to lust for her. It worked. Of course, you know what transpired after that. I even convinced David to have Bathsheba's husband killed.' Satan let out a raucous laugh. 'I felt for sure it was the end of him and God's favor toward him. Ha! David, as correctly stated in the Bible, was a man after God's own heart. God loved him. David repented oh shame the poor man did he repent. He would never build the temple to God as God promised that the sword would never leave David's kingdom due to the blood that stuck to it. Once again I was convinced that it was all said and done. David would surely never regain any power or authority again. God's punishment was that the child they bore out of deceit died, and I gave myself a high five as you say these days. I was so proud of myself. Sadly that was shortly lived as God forgave David and accepted his repentance and gave them another son. This one was the greatest king of all, besides God of course. Solomon was born, and when the time was right, all he requested from God was wisdom. I mean, come on, wisdom! He could've asked for wealth and power just as I tried to convince him to do, but he still went for wisdom. Naturally, God was very chuffed with him and gave it to him. You think you are clever or that you have clever people in this world today. Think again. That Solomon was exceptionally wise. You get clever people, and then you get wise people that always know the right decision to make; well he was wiser than them. I tried in vain to create a war between Solomon's kingdom, but God toyed with me. He kept all the other countries busy fighting each other that Solomon's kingdom reigned in peace and tranquility for forty years, and Solomon built the temple during this period; well it was indescribable in its splendor. There has never existed its equal. I had to destroy this status quo. I then went to the leaders and whispered in their ears that the country should divide into a North and South. They agreed easily, and it was so. God allowed the North to keep fighting on and off, but He kept the South at peace, this He did so that God's plan; the one and only Saviour would come from the house of David. It made me crazy. I had to wait for many, many years to finally get the South at war. The South eventually moved away from God through Solomon's sons, sons.'

'There was this one time I almost gave up my vengeful fight against God, and that was when God paused time so that Joshua was able to defeat the Amorites. He made the sun stand still over Gibeon, and the Moon stand still over Ajalon. A miraculous wonder I will never forget and be amazed by.'

'The South was eventually destroyed by Nebuchadnezzar. I man after my own heart I tell you.' Satan laughed at his irony.

'Nebuchadnezzar destroyed that temple. What a fantastic sight to see those walls crumble.' Satan gloated.

'The battle won but not my war against God. His people once again became slaves and removed from the country. A prophet Jeremiah prophesied that God's people would be free after seventy years of captivity, exactly seventy years it was so. Cyrus, the Greek king, gave them everything they needed to rebuild the temple that of course, they did. However, it never regained that same glory.

Chapter Eighteen

Jonathan shuffled in his seat, sitting for so long had made his bum a little numb, and during the movement, he happened to look at the large studio clock. Time had pressed on speedily; six o'clock was rapidly approaching. Satan too looked at the clock and grunted.

'There was so much more I wanted to tell you, but now I will have to push on. So let me get to the interesting part. Throughout the years, I kept on with my war against all that was good and righteous, many times I was so close to destroying everything when God whipped it out from under me again. But God grew weary of His people that continually disobeyed Him all because of me, and He knew it was time to bring the change that would save all of mankind. The old laws were not sufficient to save them.'

Jonathan sat up with interest quickly gulping down more water.

'Jesus was born. For thirty-three years, he roamed around just like any other boy and man, but he was blameless and a really good man.' Satan paused in thought for a few seconds.

'At the time of the Passover feast Jesus began teaching in the synagogues and temples, the people were astounded at His wisdom. He was just a boy then, but I had to make sure everyone knew that he was simply a carpenter's son and not the Messiah they were all promised.

When the time was right for Jesus' ministry to begin, He went to the wilderness for forty days. Surely I could tempt Him there while He was hungry and alone. Not Jesus - No! He sent me packing. A lot of Jews believed me. However, as you know, Jesus found His disciples, and they spread the word throughout the world that He had come to save them. Now remember they did not have the Bible then, and it was difficult to get people to believe Him until he started with all those miracles. Jeepers how do you not believe when you see a blind man see for the first time in his life or a man's disease leave him or – and the best – make a dead man alive again. Those were powerful things Jesus performed, and it was incredulous to behold. I was madly jealous, but I was able to still keep some people disbelieving. I was lucky enough to take hold of the Pharisees, Sadducees and the likes of them and when I got Jesus arrested and they way the treated Him by flogging Him and beating Him till His flesh tore, I was well pleased with myself. With regards to the flogging, do you know they only flogged Him thirty-nine times and not forty? In doing so, they kept the law rather than honoring the Messiah, who was in their presence, thirty-nine times was supposedly a merciful flogging because the Romans said that if you flogged a man forty times, he would die, but Jesus had to be crucified. I tell you I got so much pleasure watching Him being beaten up. I had the mob so energized it was just too easy. Can you believe they let that Barabbas man, a barbaric murderer, go free?' Satan burst out in a loud laugh causing Jonathan to close his ears for fear they would burst.

'Then Jesus with His beautiful crown of thorns on His head was made to carry His cross all the way to Golgotha, but they had to get that other fellow Simon to help. When Jesus hung on the cross, I relished every second. You must realize, I was trying to force Jesus to use the ten thousand angels at His disposal to destroy the world. In doing so I'd make God out to be a liar, and that would cause all creation; Hell and Earth to cease to exist and then I'd get spared the pain and misery.

I watched as the air deflated from His lungs and He had to struggle to breathe. How the pain of trying to hold Himself up was too unbearable and the blood poured from His wounds was like sweet nectar to my thoughts. I thought I had won and had finally defeated God. Jesus could have called twelve legions to take Him off that cross and destroy the world, but He hung there between two criminals. I stood by with my fingers crossed waiting for my chance to rule the universe because God would be the liar as He would not have fulfilled His promise and the universe would disintegrate and become null and void, and I would rather have had that than to spend eternity in Hell. But I failed once more, at the ultimate defeat of God. God fulfilled every promise and raised Jesus, and He reigns with Him in Heaven, interceding for all of those who truly believe in Him.'

Jonathan sat glued to his seat; his eyes were wide as saucers.

'I was not going to stop there, as long as I had time to walk among the living on earth I could still dethrone God. I believed it. I started my new plan because God was so specific about eternal salvation and how to obtain it that I used that.'

Jonathan quickly interrupted him 'Which is?'

'Confess, repent, and be baptized. Let me explain; Confess Jesus as the Saviour and the Son of God, repent of your sins and be Baptized into Jesus and be reborn a new person free from sin. You see Jesus died for your sins; He was the sacrifice. In the Old Testament law, they had to sacrifice every year, and it was a lamb, but how can a lamb wash away sins, so Jesus became the Lamb to die for your sins. Then when you come out of the water of baptism, you are too resurrected into a new life with Jesus just as the resurrection of Jesus out of the grave. Simple hey! I had to react to this hastily, so I told the guards at Jesus' grave to tell the Jews He had not risen. At least, I managed to rob hundreds of people the true knowledge that Jesus had risen and that He is the Messiah. Now I had to dilute the command of baptism. I let them believe the sprinkling of water on a baby's head was sufficient, when in fact, sprinkling does separate you from Jesus and the death, burial and the resurrection. How can a six-month-old baby repent?' Satan let out a raucous laugh.

'I put in the minds of people and in today's world - it is not that difficult - that if they touched the TV, they would be saved, or you just had to pray or say you believed, and you would have eternal life. I made the two most profitable businesses mine; the first was drug dealers and the second was the preachers of my church. You see many people and perhaps even the preachers themselves believe they are in God's church but, in fact, they are in mine. I have caused all these things to draw people away from serving God; like – greediness over money among those in the leadership of the Church, abuse of God's name, woman are meant to be silent in God's worship service, and now you have them even preaching. The use of musical instruments during worship service; oh my, the young are so influential it was so easy to change a church service into a rock concert, and they all think it is called worshipping – it's hilarious.' Satan giggled as far as he could giggle.

'I created havoc in the world too to keep people from believing the word of God. I set it into the minds of humans that the constitutions were more important than the word of God. Brutal punishments for Christians in certain parts of the world, I lured people away from thinking that baptism is the only way to Heaven, you will believe this lie because you did not heed the Word, which is the Bible – and it is the only way by the way. I split congregations and caused mankind to create all these different denominations, and the best of all was to play around with the matter of human rights and same-sex marriages. I mean that is an abomination to God, and yet you all fell for it because I whispered into a few influential people's ears that it is acceptable. And don't forget those influential people had a whack load of money to buy their way into the leaders of the world. There were just too few good people that did nothing for a lot of bad people. Now there is nothing wrong with being wealthy, but the wealthy are supposed to support the poor but I let them think they should rather want more wealth, and now they revel in their wealth only wanting more and more, and the poor remain destitute.' Satan paused a second for recollection.

'I loved placing it into people's minds that the Bible is not the word of God but in fact just a book somebody wrote.'

'Is it?' Jonathan, realizing that he would require baptism interrupted Satan.

'Oh, it is truly the word of God, and should be revered without a doubt.' Satan smiled.

'But I tempt, ensnare, devour, take captive, hinder, I am the father of liars, I oppress, and I fill man's heart with hatred.' Satan sat in silent contemplation for a few moments. His face changed into anger when he remembered the next tidbit he wanted to share.

'I was enraged when they changed the paganistic festival to 25th December, Christmas day. My festival! My festival! My!' Satan slammed his fist down on the arm of the chair breaking it into splinters. He watched in amusement as Jonathan's arm flew up to cover and protects his face.

Chapter Nineteen

'So now you know all about me and what I have done to the world.'

With his lips quivering and his throat congested Jonathan squeaked out 'Why have you revealed all of this? Why give away all your secrets?'

Satan's face becomes extremely downcast and mournful 'Just wait....' Satan sighs sadly. 'I am defeated, and all I can do is reveal the truth for once in my existence, and maybe now, people will listen to me since they don't want to listen to God, their creator.'

Jonathan's body wanted to run from the chair and find a church to get baptized, but he couldn't move for fear that Satan would zap him as he did with Alex.

'You can only leave the studio once the show begins to air. You have to wait until after the editing of the interview. I don't see why you should have an advantage over anyone else do you?'

Jonathan just shook his head, everything inside of him was screaming for him to make a run for it, but fear kept him seated. There was a rattle at the door and then a knock. Both Satan and Jonathan turned to look at the door. Jonathan looked at Satan for an answer as to what he was supposed to do.

'Go and let them in.'

When Jonathan opened the door there stood all the editing staff, the producer and Mr. Eckenberg waiting with very curious faces to enter. When they laid their eyes on Jonathan, they were instantly shocked at his appearance. He was sweating profusely, and his eyes were bloodshot from his tears as well as the heat from the portal to hell.

'Jonathan. What's wrong?' Mr. Eckenberg asked as they all moved forward toward the control room.

Jonathan merely shook his head 'Oh it's been a long morning without any sleep.' He did not want to hurry them on as it would be suspicious and the last thing he felt like doing right now was answering questions he was not allowed to answer.

Satan had disappeared from his chair when Jonathan returned to the set. The staff filled their mugs with coffee and settling into their usual pace before actually getting started with the editing. Jonathan was about to explode out of his skin he was so impatient and on edge.

Mr. Eckenberg requested that Jonathan join them in the control room, but Jonathan declined. He was too nervous to stand in that confined space and besides that was one interview he never wanted to relive again – ever.

The staff got going and as they worked their easy disposition changed into a tensed concern. Jonathan hovered around the exit doors ready to make a run for it as soon as the editing was over.

During this time, adverts were being aired around the world. The headlines on each and every TV, on every network and every channel shouted "Exclusive special interview with the devil on The Bale Show."

As the interview rolled along Jonathan could hardly bear it no more, he sat on the floor and sobbed. His body shook violently as the dread of knowing overtook his senses.

In the control room, the staff were glued to the TV screens, their teeth began to rattle, and the sweat poured off their brows as the truth was unveiled to them. Mr. Eckenberg unable to stand it any longer, dashed out of the control room terrified and screaming.

He reached Jonathan still crying on the floor and as Jonathan looked up at him and their eyes connected, reflecting the same fear, Satan zapped Mr. Eckenberg.

He shouted out in horror, and severe pain then fizzled into red burning dust before Jonathan's eyes. Satan called from somewhere in the walls 'No one is to leave until it's over.'

Jonathan screeched in agony and absolute terror writhing in fear and despair on the floor.

At eleven o'clock exactly the show without the aid of anyone in the control room began to air on the TVs all over the world. The staff were mesmerized to the seats, too afraid to move or budge. Their tears flowed uncontrollably.

Chapter Twenty

As the interview continued the TV people all around the world, stopped what they were doing to watch. After all, this is Jonathan Bale, and if he was hosting a special broadcast, it had to be something spectacular.

As the interview progressed worldwide panic slowly ensued as people realized how wrong they had been and that there is, in fact, a God, and He had given a definite command for entry into Heaven, written in His Word the Bible.

Jonathan crumbled at the exit door begging Satan to let him go. He heard a click and stopped sobbing enough to hear Satan say to him 'Go!' Satan threw out his outrageous laughter and vanished from sight and sound.

Jonathan scrambled to his feet; they were like jelly, and he struggled to walk let alone run. He leaned against the walls of the building to get to his car. It was a struggle for him to press the button of the electronic remote to open his car door. As he tried to get the key into the ignition he yelled at himself to calm down; he was too out of control to even obey himself. By sheer luck, he got the key in and started the car. His legs were shaking so shoddily changing gears was almost impossible. He had no coordination, and in desperation, he pulled out of his parking lot in whatever gear he found first. He crashed his car into the cars alongside him but cared not and sped out of the parking garage.

He raced down the road shouting 'Get out the way! Help me! Where is a Church! Oh please help me, God!'

His phone vibrated in his pocket, and the call appeared on the car radio panel. It was Cassia.

'Babe where are you, we are watching this interview, we are so scared; please come home. Please, babe, come home.' Cassia sobbed as she begged her husband to go home to her and their children.

'Save yourself.' Jonathan cried back to the radio still racing down the road.

As he flung the car around one corner after another desperately looking for a church that was open, he was aware that there were now hoards of people running about the streets yelling and screaming. They had clearly been watching the show and realized their fate. Jonathan noticed a small church down a side alley and parked his car on the sidewalk. He jumped out the car forgetting to lock or even close the door. He ran up to the entrance and saw a crowd of people begging a man to baptize them. The man refused. They begged even louder. Jonathan ran back to his car, but it was gone; stolen. He screamed at the sky and ran colliding with others with the same purpose.

As Jonathan ran passed businesses and stores he had to dodge others streaming out of the entrance doors; they too were looking to find God. Every church he passed had people banging on the doors, smashing windows to get in, kneeling in front of the church praying; churches that were preaching half-truths and whole lies!

Pandemonium had set in all over the world. Chaos was extreme, and panic, terror, and fear were rampant.

Jonathan was exhausted and running out of sheer adrenaline, crying and begging anyone to help him.

He bashed into a church, pushed his way through the crowd to the front not caring if he hurt anyone in the process or the verbal abuse flung at him. He saw they were sprinkling water on the people in a hurry to get them all done. 'That's wrong.' He yells

'It's all we can do in the mayhem,' replied the man in desperation.

'It's wrong. It's wrong. Didn't you hear what Satan said?' Jonathan shouted as he turned and bolted out of the church.

Every church he went too was overcrowded with people on the same mission. He found a church baptizing people fast and furiously; it was the Church of Christ, but the line of people was so long. He ran on looking for another church of the same name.

He stopped to take a breath and looked across the road toward a shop that had TVs in the window playing the last few minutes of the interview. Jonathan looked at Satan and crumbled to the ground. The reminder was too much for him to bear. An urge of energy overcame him, and he managed to get up and continue his search among the thousands of others for the same reprieve.

He came to several churches with Church of Christ bolded written on them, and each one had hundreds of people waiting to be baptized. Jonathan again forced his way to the front receiving the same violent reaction from the people each time. At one church, he stood in front of the minister and pleaded. "I am Jonathan Bale I know you recognize me. I did that interview. I should be baptized first. I should get priority treatment. Baptize me now then you can carry on with the others.'

The people shouted their objections at his demands. For the first time, Jonathan Bale was unable to use his name or fame to get what he wanted. For the first time since "The Bale Show" started he was treated like the enemy. No one cared who he was anymore. He was now just like any other human being.

'I'm afraid you will have to get into the line like everyone else. We are all equal in the eyes of God, and you are no exception.'

'But I…' He started to raise his objections when the line of people quickly became a mob and physically forced him out the church. Jonathan cursed and objected in vain.

He was panicking that he was unable to use his fame for self-gain and continued to search for someone to baptize him.

He staggered in and out of so many churches, the ones open were inundated with scrambling panicking people waiting in a line as long as a mile.

He ran past a park noticing a woman sitting peacefully on the ground smiling. He looked at her intently confused as to why she acted so differently to everyone else. Wanting to go and speak to her curious as to why she acted so differently he slowed his pace and made his way to her. As he turned a mob of hysterical people knocked him over in their pursuit to find salvation. Jonathan stood up cursing them in loud, obscene profanity. Still in the process of yelling; another group of anxious people came pouring past him, dragging him with them. There was no way to turn around or change direction as groups of people became masses. The wailing, crying, screaming, reached such intensity it was impossible to hear their thoughts.

Jonathan ran around aimlessly reduced to the stature of a normal person begging for mercy.

He thought of his family and cried. But his selfish, arrogant nature had now left him alone among strangers while his beautiful wife held her children in her bosom.

Cassia sobbed uncontrollably.

The woman sitting on the grass in the park somehow void of being run over by the mobs of people sat peacefully with her eyes closed looking up to Heaven. She prayed continually smiling. Her face was a light of joy.

Chapter Twenty-One

Worldwide hysteria reigned in every country, some unfortunately during the darkness of night, others through snow, rain, hail, dust storms, heat, hurricanes but all were subjected to the same event.

Jonathan floundered through streets, alleys, and parks searching along with the rest of the world for someone who cared enough to baptize him.

For a second there was a deathly silence, a quiet before the storm as if the world required a pause for something great that was about to happen - it was!

The sun darkened not to black but to an unusual shade never seen before by mankind. Loud sounds were haunting the people of the world from the skies. At first, the consensus was that it was thunder, but it soon became too loud even for that. Their ears could bear it no longer, and people fell like flies to the ground covering their ears for mercy.

When the sound lessened, a heavy white, very white, too bright to look at, cloud formed low down and hovered above the earth. The dense intensity of the cloud pushed everyone downward, and people shuddered on the ground crying and pleading for mercy. Some, among them, was Linda, sat on the ground and smiled in awe and wonder and excitement.

And suddenly there was ear deafening loud trumpet sounds in the heavens. All the people of earth looked up.

It is the second coming of Christ.

Many, many, people did not have a chance at repentance for they had rather listened to Satan for a few hours and believed him; than listen to God for more than two thousand years.

Soon what seemed to be an apparition appeared through the cloud, brighter than the cloud itself, that the people turned their faces to the ground fearing permanent blindness. A loud voice resounded, and instantly many smaller spirits - angels, not so white came floating to earth.

If ever Jonathan had been afraid of what he had seen and heard in the past few hours, nothing was compared to what he saw right then. Graves opened, and souls of people lifted skyward. Jonathan and people around him screamed for mercy that God would be merciful to them as the souls of many floated past them. For the longest time, this went on; suddenly living people began to rise and float towards God. The angels instructed by God floated about lifting those selected and chosen to live for eternity with Him. As they elevated to the sky, they were transformed into God's likeness.

Those rejected on the earth stretched out their arms in hysteria beseeching forgiveness.

Jonathan; already been privy to his eternal death, as the images of the portal to hell flung to the forefront of his mind, was unable to do anything but cry in shame and sorrow. He looked momentarily at Linda, still smiling, and watched how she was lifted up and became an image of God.

What seemed to be an eternity of watching the faithful servants of God be raised and welcomed into His arms ended.

Another silence hung heavily for a few seconds before Satan stood before Jonathan. Satan laughed, and Jonathan cried.

"Not everyone who says to me, 'Lord, Lord,' will enter the kingdom of heaven, but the one who does the will of my Father, who is in heaven.
On that day, many will say to me, 'Lord, Lord, did we not prophesy in your name, and cast out demons in your name, and do mighty works in your name?
And then I will declare to them, 'I never knew you; depart from me, you workers of lawlessness.'"

Matthew 7: 21 – 23

Your Opinion

You've come to the end of this story; I truly hope you enjoyed it and it touched your heart.

Please be kind and leave your review for the benefit of the many to follow, I will be so appreciative.

https://www.amazon.com/day-God-came-earth-ebook/dp/B0195NCV2C/

Thank you
God bless you

Aileen Friedman

More Books By The Author

Aileen Friedman

Changes From a Sunset
ISBN   978-0-620-52564-0

When is My Forever
ISBN   978-0-620-55793-1

Second is Best
ISBN   978-0-620-59758-6

The Sparkle in Her Eyes plus Six more Short Stories
ISBN   978-0-620-64434-1

Radar Love
ISBN   978-1-543-29950-2

The Secret of Grace
ISBN   978-1-719-17242

Mr. Trolley Adventurer
ISBN   978-1-533-27328-4

Jamie's Discoveries
ISBN   978-1-533-27339-0